Dear MERCY

Enjoy this Book as
much as I enjoyed
writing it.

[signature]

WONDRICUS

Children and the adults who read it alone or with them will love **Wondricus - The Quest for the Way Out**. They are sure to laugh and wonder while they nod at the wisdom imparted within the story.

Wondricus is a marvellous tale of a children's adventure fantasy in the land where rainbows are born. It is whimsical like Alice in Wonderland, Peter Pan and The Wizard of Oz.

If there is a pot of gold at the end of the rainbow. What is at the beginning?

Two resourceful children accidentally float away tied to a cluster of balloons. While drifting in the air, they dodge a dangerous woodpecker and save a one-legged bird with only five wings before they trip on a rainbow.

Sliding down on the slippery blue band of the rainbow they land in the florest of Runkledungding where they meet a wise and helpful elf. There are no trees in the florest. If there were, it would be a forest. The florest is filled with gigantic flowers and inhabited by strange and wonderful animals.

As they explore this strange land, the children encounter many extraordinary creatures like the kangadrool who may be terrified of kangaroos; the crocosmile who owns a watch that can speed or slow time depending on his mood; the ant sniffer who sniff ants because he is an ant sniffer; the balamoose who holds up his antlers with suspenders; the horse of a feather who does not stick together and the zoom-by who gets so excited he can hardly zoom still. They also skilfully dodge the inept giant nasty tertiums who want to kidnap them to make a bouquet to give their mother on her birthday.

Once they reach Rainbow Falls the children witness the fantastic birth of a rainbow. They also cleverly discover the secret magical way to return to their home.

The story has much humour and some light suspense but is without violence.

Chapters are short and highly suitable for bedtime story reading.

Wondricus

The Search for the Way Out!

Pierre Lalonde

Illustration
Gary Frederick

Wondricus
© Pierre Lalonde
© Wondricus Publishing
ISBN 9798732215342
All Rights Reserved including newly created words.
3rd Edition

Dedicated to Patricia, William and Simon with Love.

Grandchildren are the true source of rainbows. They should also be their destinations.

There are Marlavous and wondricus things
That live in the Florest of Ronkledongding.
There is a one-legged bird with only five wings
And there's a great big rock that won't do a thing.

If you want to know:

- *How to fly in the air!*
- *How to fool a woodpecker while floating in the air tied to balloons!*
- *How an elf doctor cures children by making them smile!*
- *What happens when a kangadrool hops on a crocosmile's tail!*
- *Why antsniffers do not eat ants!*
- *Why lovers wear yellow plastic helmets!*
- *What is the taste of a choconut!*
- *How fast can a zoom-by can run!*
- *How can a horse of a feather stick together!*
- *How dangerous nastytertiums can be!*
- *How to transform nastytertiums into niceytertiums!*
- *The secret password to enter Rainbow Falls!*
- *How rainbowsare made!*
- *How to ride on a rainbow!*

Turn the page and read!

A Visit to the Fair

I think that you are ready to hear the extraordinary adventure of "The Search for the Way Out".

This adventure began quite a while ago. About as long ago as it takes to wait for Christmas to come - plus the time it takes to wait for a birthday to come - multiplied by the time it takes to find out whether you have been found out when you deserve to be in trouble – in a great big mess of trouble. Yes, that long ago, plus three hours and five minutes - not an ordinary five minutes. A five minute as long as a child has to wait when a busy parent says: "yes dear, I'll be with you in five more minutes".

We all know how long that is!

That long ago, there were two wonderful children. The boy was Emorix and the girl was Coral. Their parents were very loving and very supportive. Their mother took good care of them and gave them good advice. She taught them how to be polite. The father loved them very much. He spent a lot of time telling the mother to take good care of the children.

The father was a funny kind of man, just like most fathers are. He had a tendency to do just a bit too much for his children. They were happy children. Sometimes they had troubles, like when they did not get a third cookie or when they had to go to bed before "too late". But besides that, the children were happy.

One sunny summer day, a circus and a big fair came to their town. The father was very excited. He hardly slept the night before the fair. At three minutes before "much too early in the morning", he started making little noises hoping the children would wake up. They did not wake up. He made more little noises. He made some bigger noises. He snored and snorted like three elephants whose trunks were all tied up. Still the children did not wake up.

The mother who was wise to the father's tricks said: "Stop it. Let the children sleep." He became quiet for seven and a half seconds. Then he shouted: "Oh my god! We overslept. Everybody, wake up. It's almost noon."

The mother whispered: "Quiet! It is still way before wake up time".

Mothers like to say things like that. But it was too late. Mokka, the dog who always believed what the father said, was awake. She hopped out of bed and went to nudge the children. She licked their face. That did it. The children woke up and smiled. The children sensed a new adventure. There was always something special when their father woke them up before "too early". They hardly had time to make their bed when the mother guessed the reason for the father's excitement. She said: "Maybe we should go to the fair today".

"Is there a fair?" Said the father trying to look surprised.

"Yes! Yes!" Said the children.

"Well mother, I think you had a good idea. I wish I had thought of it myself". Said the father, unable to hide his excitement. "Okay, that's decided - We leave in three minutes. Let's go!" He shouted as he leapt towards the door.

The mother yelled: "Come back here. You are worse than the children. You are still in your pajamas. The fair is not even open yet. We will have breakfast and leave in time to still be the first to arrive at the fair."

Coral and Emorix were used to that routine. They smiled at each other as they ate their breakfast. They ate all of it. Another exiting day was about to begin.

At the fair their dad bought them cotton candy and candied apples. He also bought some for himself so the children would not feel alone when they ate. He also took them on all the rides except the Supersonic Upside-Down Bumping Whirler and the Backward Hiccuping Rolling and Twirling Coaster. He said he wanted to stay on the ground to take pictures of the children and their mother on those rides. He thought the pictures would look nice in the picture album - right beside the ones he took last year of the mother and the children on the same rides. The children winked and smiled at each other as they got on the rides with their mother. They waved to their father who waited bravely and safely on the ground.

After the rides they had lunch. They had pistachio bubble gum flavored chocolate sundaes for dessert.

After lunch, their father bought them great big balloons. It was the kind of balloons that are filled with helium gas, so they float up in the air. You tie them to your wrist, so they don't fly away. An ordinary father would have bought one or two balloons for each child. But a father who is more a child than his children did not stop at one or two balloons. Every time the mother was not looking, he kept buying more and more balloons. He bought red ones, blue ones and yellow ones. He bought balloons that looked like dogs and a great big one that looked like a three-scoop ice cream cone. When he tied the three-scoop ice cream cone balloon to the children's wrist - big troubles began. The children felt lighter and lighter on their feet. Finally, with a big gust of wind, they were blown away and kept rising higher and higher.

At first the children were not as worried as their mother was. The father kept yelling for them to come back right now. That did not help very much. Mokka, the dog also barked for them to come back. That almost helped, but it did not.

The wind grew stronger, and the children got higher. They soon were too high to be rescued by the tallest ladder of the fire truck - the one that had rushed in to rescue them. They were too high for the ladder even when the fire truck drove up the hill. Not that it would have helped. The hill was in the wrong place. The children were floating over the valley. They could not be rescued with a helicopter. The rotor blades would have burst the balloons.

At first Emorix and Coral were worried. There were still a few rides that they would have liked to try again.

The Children knew they would not fall to the ground unless the balloons broke. That was unlikely. Their father had bought only the best balloons. He had bought those high-quality balloons that don't break easily. Nothing was too good for his children.

Emorix and Coral were together. They decided to hold hand to make sure they would not drift apart. They held on to their cotton candy floss and all the other food that their father had bought them. They might get hungry later.

They decided to make the best of it and enjoy the flight. They recognized their house and their school as they flew over. They even waved as they passed their grandmother's house. She waved back blowing kisses at them while wondering why they were flying so high like that.

They kept going South at a very fast rate. Just as they were about to reach the town limits. An airplane pulling a banner passed in front of them. There was a message for them on the banner. It said: "Take care, we will follow you. We will save you as soon as we can - Love from mother and father."

They liked that. It was the first time that a plane had a message written specially for them.

The wind was steady and fast. Sometimes it went Southeast. Sometimes it went Southwest. Most of the time the wind blew towards the South. They drifted like that for many days. It is a good thing that their dad had bought them too much cotton candy, too many candied apples and too many bags of peanuts. They did not get hungry.

They had only one problem. They did not know where to put the red cardboard cones from the cotton candy they had eaten. They did not know where to put the peanut shells. Their mother had thought them not to be litter bugs. Coral, who was pretty smart, had a good idea. She tied the cones to the balloon strings. She and Emorix carefully put the peanut shells inside the cones. That solved the litter problem. It also made their balloon cluster look much prettier. Sometimes the wind would blow into the cones and make a pretty whistling noise. It was like having a radio in a car. Except that it was not a radio. It was cardboard horns tied to a bunch of balloons.

On the third day, there was another problem. A great big woodpecker came very close to their balloons. Perhaps it was the whistling sound from the cones that attracted it. Sometimes it sounded like the wind blowing through the trees. The children were afraid that the woodpecker would try to peck at the balloons. That would be dangerous. Emorix always had a plan when he needed one. He thought of a great plan. He started to sing: "Row, row, row your boat gently down the stream..." Coral joined in.

That fooled the woodpecker. Woodpeckers are easy to fool. They are not very smart. That is why they peck at trees to eat bugs instead of eating apple pie and ice cream.

Everyone, especially woodpecker watchers, knows that woodpeckers, never attack boats. The woodpecker thought that if Emorix and Coral were singing that song, surely, they were on a boat. The woodpecker was fooled. He flew away looking for trees to peck. Maybe he was also looking for other children drifting away hanging on a bunch of balloons. Maybe he went looking for children who did not think of singing about rowing a boat.

On the fourth day, the wind became strange. It blew faster. Sometimes it blew up. Other times it blew down. It is a good thing that the children were experienced at riding the Supersonic Upside-Down Bumping Whirler and the Backward Hiccuping Rolling and Twirling Coaster. Had they not, they would have been scared. The wind pushed the children and the floating balloons towards a rainbow. They could see the pot of gold at the end of it.

Another bird came towards them. It was the strangest bird that they had ever seen. It was yellow and blue and red and pink and had a golden beak. It also had a tail made of long rags. It looked like the tail of a kite. It was flying forward. It was flying sideways, and it was flying backward. It was flying as if it had the hiccups. They had never seen a bird fly like that. The bird looked in their direction and came closer to them. They could see that it had only one leg. But the bird had five wings.

Is that not the strangest bird you have ever seen? What kind of bird is it?

Emorix and Coral started to sing: "Row, row, row your boat".

The bird came closer and said: "You are silly, you are not on a boat, you are near the rainbow. Everybody knows that rainbows are not boats. What are you doing so high?"

The children told their story to the bird.

The bird said: "This is interesting. I have never heard of a pistachio bubble gum flavored chocolate sundae. What does it taste like? Myself, I prefer fun flower seeds".

The children told the bird that pistachio bubble gum flavored chocolate sundaes tasted almost as good as pistachio bubble gum flavored chocolate sundaes with seven cherries on top. They could see the bird licking its beak. They could hear its stomach squeaking. Bird stomachs do not growl. They squeak.

"You also have only one leg." Said Coral. "Did you have a bad accident?"

The bird replied: "Oh no - that is a good thing. It is a good thing to have only one leg. When I am near the ground, I live on telephone poles. The poles are so far apart that if I had two legs, I would have to stretch my legs too far to put one leg on each of two poles. That would hurt. With only one leg, I need to be on only one pole, I don't have to stretch at all - that is much better."

The bird continued: "Maybe you can help me. I have great trouble. You see I have only five wings: one wing to fly up, one wing to fly backward, one wing to fly forward, one wing to fly to the left and one wing to fly to the right. I don't have a wing to fly down. I keep going higher and higher. I am afraid that one day I will bump my head on the moon. I have been up here for so many years that I forgot my birthday. I am even afraid that another bird may have taken my telephone pole."

The children thought about what the bird had said. It was very much like the trouble they were in. Then Coral explained to the bird that he did not need a wing to go down. Rocks go down when you throw them in the air and rocks don't have wings. Maybe if the bird did not use any wings at all he would go down. All he had to do was to be careful. When he got close to the ground, he could use his "up wing" to slow down his fall. After that, he could use his left going wing to stop going up. He would be so close to the ground that he could let himself fall softly for the last little bit.

The bird smiled. He thought it was a good idea. He thanked the children. He closed all his wings and pointed his head towards the ground. He began to fall faster and faster. The children were worried that he would not stop in time. They were afraid that he would splash too hard on the ground. Just as he came very close to squash his head on a big rock, the bird opened his up-going wing. He stopped falling. Before he could begin to rise too high again, he closed the up-going wing and opened his left-going wing to stabilize his fall. The children finally saw him close his wings again and fall softly to the ground. They heard laughter in the distance. They knew that their new friend was happy to be back where he lived. The children felt good about that.

At the Beginning of the Rainbow

Soon, things got complicated. The wind blew harder and pushed the children very quickly towards the rainbow. No matter how hard they tried; they could not go over or go under the rainbow. The balloons were floating too high to go under and the children had eaten too much to go clearly over. As they crossed the rainbow, their feet tripped in the blue band of the rainbow. Two things happened. First, the tripping made them flip upside down. Second, after the flip, they started sliding on the back of the rainbow - on the same blue band that had tripped them.

The blue band of the rainbow is the slipperiest of all the bands. The children were sliding very fast - faster than on a roller coaster. Emorix was the first to notice that they were sliding away from the pot of gold. They were going towards the beginning of the rainbow.

We all know there is a pot of gold at the end of a rainbow.

Very few people know what is at the beginning of a rainbow – you are about to find out. It is a big secret. You will become one of the very few who know.

At high noon, which is better than at low noon, the balloons, the cones and the children stopped abruptly. The strings had been caught in the petal of a very strange tree; it looked like a giant flower. The children hung in the air as if they were in a parachute caught in the trees. The wind and the rainbow had brought the children to a strange place. Maybe it was a good thing. Maybe it was not a good thing. One thing was certain. It was a very strange thing.

Coral said: "Wow! What a pretty place."

Emorix said: "We are very high up."

Coral said: "Look how tall the flowers are! We are in a flower."

Emorix said: "They can't be flowers, They are too big."

Coral said: "They look like flowers and they smell like flowers, they must be flowers."

Emorix said: "It is a good thing that dad is not here. He would want us to pick a bouquet to give to mother. Wow! That would be hard work"

Coral said: "Don't joke, I wish both mother and father were here with us."

Emorix said: "I am not sure we should wish they were here with us. Perhaps it would be better to wish we were there with them! This is a very strange place. I have never seen anything like it. I have never even heard of a place like this one. Oh - it worries me"

Coral said: "What is this place anyway?"

"It is the Florest of Ronkledongding."

"Thank you," said Emorix: "How did you know that?"

"Know what?" said Coral.

"Know that it is the Forest of Runkessomething." Said Emorix.

Coral looked a little confused... she said: "Well! You just told me."

"No." Said Emorix who was also puzzled. "You told me". He spoke.

"I did no such thing, I wonder..."

Both children had the same suspicion at the same time. They were not alone! There was someone else, scary?

They both looked down and saw a very strange person. He looked a bit like a short and very old man. He seemed very kind. He also looked a bit like an elf. His face was a bit like that of a person but then it was not. He had ears like a bunny and his nose was round and twitchy. He also wore the uniform of a policeman. The dominant feature were the two smiles on his face. Two smiles? Yes, there was a big grin on his mouth but there was also a bigger smile in his eyes. He was looking up at them. There was something magical in the smiling twinkle in his eyes. The children did not know whether he was an elf or a person – perhaps he was an "Elfperson" or a "Personelf" Whatever, the children immediately sensed he was a friendly old man. Their parents had told them not to talk to strangers. Normally they would not, but this was a special occasion and a special stranger who was a police officer. They were lost in a very strange land. They were far away from home in a place that was like nothing they had ever heard before. Maybe they were in danger. They needed a friend to help and guide them. The kindly old policeman below them looked ready to help. They did not need to think about it very much. They had found a policeman to help them. There was nothing phony and nothing threatening about this short smiling elf-like person and there was nothing else they could do.

"Is it all right if we come down?" Said Coral, who had learned to be polite from her mother.

"Of course, it is. Be careful." Said the old man. "It is even better if you come down than if you do not. Actually, if you do not come down, there is a danger that you may fall down faster than any of the three of us would want. You must have had a long trip. You are probably very tired. It would be good if you came down rather than fell down."

Both children thought that this was a wise thing. But how would they do it? Hanging high from the top of the giant flower was a challenge. The strings of the balloons would not reach all the way to the ground.

It is a good thing that Emorix was always ready to think of new plan. He was good at that. Once he had made a plan for a birdhouse that he built with his father. The birds would have really enjoyed their new house had his father drilled an entrance hole at the front of the birdhouse like the hole Emorix's plan required. Instead, sadly some silly birds bumped their head on the wall trying to get inside the pretty bird house that did not have an entrance. This time Emorix needed an even better plan. He would have needed to dig very deep in his bag of tricks - only if he had brought his bag of tricks with him. The bag of tricks was still at home. It was neatly put away in his toy box.

Both Emorix and Coral thought very hard. Then, they had an idea. They could climb down on a ladder. But they did not have a ladder. They asked the old man for one - but he did not have one either.

Then they remembered that they had started climbing only when there were many balloons tied to their wrist. Even then, the balloon salesman, who was holding many more balloons than the children, had not floated in the air. He had not floated in the air because he was bigger and heavier. Had he been smaller and lighter he would have floated in the air just like the children did.

If he had been holding many more balloons he would also have floated in the air, even as big as he was. That thinking got the children to develop a really smart plan. They were afraid that if they let one balloon go, they would come down too fast and hurt themselves. But what if they gained weight? That would make them heavier. The heavier they became, the harder it would be for the balloons to hold them up. They wanted to float down slowly. The idea was to gain weight slowly. Now that they had a plan, they had to think how to make it work.

They had many choices. They could wait until they grew up. Grownups are heavier. That was a good way to gain weight, but it would take too much time.

Another way would be to eat until they got fatter. That also would take too much time and too much food.

They had to think of a better way. Weight does not have to be inside you. A person carrying a stone has more weight than before he picked it up. That person would get even heavier if he picked up another stone.

That was it! They would pick up weight - a little bit at a time - until they became just a little too heavy for the balloons. Then they would float down. If they fell too fast, they could drop some weight. That was it. They had found the way to get down safely. They looked around them. They picked some of the seeds from the flower. The seeds were very big. They were as big as a very large apple. Five seeds, nothing happened. Ten seeds - still nothing ... they had to place some in the cones, fifteen seeds - no changes, but when they had twenty-two seeds, the balloons started going down very slowly. They drifted downward. It took a long while, but gently, as if they were in a helicopter but without the noise, they drifted towards the ground.

The lower they got, the more they could see the old man's wrinkled smile and the sparkle in his eyes. They even thought that the closer they got to him the more he smiled.

The old policeman had watched how the children had worked together. He had seen how they had figured out how to solve their problem on their own. He liked what he had seen. He looked forward to making friends with the children. He looked forward to helping them.

"I am Coral, and this is my brother Emorix, who are you?"

"I am Standor." He said. "Nice to meet you".

"Please tell us, where did you say we were?"

"You are in the Florest of Ronkledongding."

"The forest of Ronkledongding?" said Emorix.

"No, not the Forest of Ronkledongding. If it were a forest there would be trees. These are flowers. It is a florest."

That made a lot of sense to the children.

The Florest of Ronkledongding.

You probably have never heard of the Florest of Runkledongding. Let me tell you what Standor told the children about it.

There are marlavous and wondricus things
that live in the Florest of Ronkledongding.
There is a one-legged bird with only five wings
and there's a great big rock that won't do a thing.

The Florest of Ronkledongding has no trees. If it had, it would be a forest, not a florest. It is a florest because it is full of flowers - very special flowers. They are gigantical and excitraordinary flowers.

In the Florest of Ronkledongding there are flowers as big as "bigger". Being as big as bigger makes the flowers bigger than most trees. We all know that only the biggest of the biggest trees get to grow as big as "bigger". They never grow bigger than that.

In the Florest of Ronkledongding there are many kinds of giant flowers. The "forget me nuts" flowers are so big that, if you saw them, you would never forget them. You would remember them forever.

There are many other kinds of flowers. There are the "Chrysemtemaximums" and the "truelips". These are even bigger than the biggest of the forget me nuts.

There are also "fun flowers". The seeds of the fun flowers are very tasty. Birds love to eat them. The shell of the fun flower seed is very strong. It is very thick. I think you would need an extra big and heavy hammer to open the seeds. You would need a salt mine to salt the fun flower seeds. You would need a mouth as big as a volcano's mouth to eat those seeds. Only the biggest birds, the ones with a hard and pointed beak, get to eat the fun flower seeds.

There are many other flowers in the Florest of Ronkledongding.

There are "dizzies" that have very thick petals. You would need a big chain saw to play "he loves me - he loves me not" with the dizzy petals. You would have to be very careful that the one you love was not under the dizzies when you picked the petals. To be safe, the one you love would have to wear one of those bright yellow safety hats and steel reinforced safety boots. Better, he should move away from under the dizzies. A falling petal would put a big bump on the top of his head. It would make him forget that you were there. Worse, it could make him forget that he was supposed to love you. Worse than worse - the bump on his head would make the one you love look like a one hump camel. I don't think you would love someone that looks like a one hump camel. A one hump camel is called a dromedary. That would be a funny name for someone you love.

There is another kind of flower in the florest. It is called the "potrose". Potroses have thorns so big that the "rhynoferocious" uses one thorn as a horn at the end of his snout. The rhynoferocious does not use all of the thorns because there are many thorns and there is only one rhynoferocious. He is lonely. He has no other rhynoferocious to play hopscotch with. Perhaps that is why he is so ferocious. Of course, the "rhynoferocious" could put more than one thorn at the end of his snout. He does not. That would make him look too ferocious. Also, when he comes towards someone, he could be mistaken for a "porky-U-pine backing up". The rhynoferocious is choosy. He does not want his face to look like the back end of a porky-U-pine. This makes sense. No one wants a face that looks like the back end of a porky-U-pine. Not even those who have a face that looks like the back end of a porky-U-pine. Not even porky-U-pines want a face that looks like the back end of a porky-U-pine.

The people who live in the Florest of Ronkledongding use the left-over thorns from the "potroses" to build tepees and huts. The huts and teepees keep them warm in winter and safe from attack. No one wants to attack a house that looks like the back end of a porky-U-pine. What if it was a real porky-U-pine?

There is a "beleaver" in the Florest of Ronkledongding. He has a big flat tail. He also has two big teeth that are longer than his mouth. They hang down. Sometimes they get stuck in the ground. Sometimes they don't. He likes it better when they don't. The beleaver believes that he is an engineer. He likes to build dams. The beleaver also wants to enjoy the view. He has built his dam high on top of the hill. He thinks that this way he will see as far as "away". There is a problem with building a dam on top of a hill. The beleaver has no water for his dam and no water for his lodge. He does not have water to swim in. He does not even have water to sink in.

The beleaver has hired the kangadrool to help him. The kangadrool goes down to the river and asks the "bellyfant" to fill his pouch with water. Then, hop to the top - the kangadrool goes up the hill. There, he stands upside down on his head and dumps the water from his pouch. The water that does not flow inside his nostrils fills the pond behind the dam. After seven hundred times seven hundred and three trips, there is just enough water behind the dam to make mud pies. The mud pies taste like mud. The beleaver opened a bakery to sell his mud pies. He has many customers. There is a "Hy-ho-po-tamous", some "pligs" and many "mud flarks". They line up every day to buy mud pies, mud cakes, mud balls and mud doughnuts. The mud doughnuts are the best. They have very tasty dry holes in the middle.

The beleaver is now very rich. He thinks he can afford not to have enough water behind his dam. Instead, he has bought a painting of the sea and has hung it on a wall in his lodge. Unfortunately, you can't take a bath in an oil painting. It is too oily. The bubble bath soap does not make enough bubbles to cover even his big toe. The poor beleaver lost all his friends because he was always dirty behind his ears. That makes him poorer than those who have no money but have many friends to play with. They are the rich ones. The believer has rehired the kangadrool to get more water.

There is also a "balamoose" in the Florest of Ronkledongding. He has great problems because his suspenders broke a long time ago. Without suspenders, his antlers fall to his knees. He has to be bow-legged to prevent the antlers from ripping the skin off his legs. He even wears long and thick green socks to protect his knees. He spent all his time looking for new and stronger suspenders. He finally found some last November. He hung them from the leaves of a "lolly of the volley". At first, he hung them so tight that he bounced in the air as if he was on a jolly jumper. He bounced as if he was a yo-yo. When he finished bouncing, he was hanging very high above the ground. So high that the "giantraffes" had to stand on the tip of their toes to reach up and lick his feet. They also pulled at his socks and made him go bong bong as he bounced up and down. He did not like that very much.

The balamoose has adjusted his suspenders but he is still stuck under the lolly of the volley and cannot go visit his aunts and his uncles. All he can do is walk in circles under the lolly of the volley. That can be dangerous. Sometimes he goes around too many times and wraps the suspenders too tight. The elastic pulls him back and twirls him around and around like a propeller on top of a beanie. That earned him the nickname of Whizzy. It is not a much better nickname than Bumpy - the nickname he had when he bounced up and down on his suspenders and bumped his head on the branches. The balamoose is very unhappy.

There are one thousand and two dozen "monkbees" living at the top of the flowers. They fly with their wings and flip with their tails. They chatter most of the time. They buzz the rest of the time. They make banana honey so sweet and mellow that it can make a grump smile. That's how the "crocosmile" got its name. He used to be called "crocogrump". When the crocosmile is not watching, the monkbees try to steal his "choconuts". They like to drink the cool strawberry milk that is in them.

The monkbees also like to drop the choconuts on loved ones who stand under dizzies. Those who wear big yellow safety hats and safety boots. The monkbees like the ping sound that the choconuts make as they go bump on top of the helmets. They also like the thump sound the loved ones make when they faint and fall on the ground. The monkbees are very popular. Everyone loves them - not exactly everyone. The yellow-helmeted loved ones and those who love the yellow-helmeted loved ones do not like the monkbees very much.

Standor

I don't think you have met Standor. Let me tell you a little bit about him.

Standor is wise enough to grow old and old enough to grow wise. He is also a witch doctor. Standor is a Ronkian. He is the only Ronkian who is a policeman and a witch doctor.

As a witch doctor, Standor is not busy at all. Every person who knows it - knows that there are no witches in the Florest of Ronkledongding. If there were witches, they would be very healthy witches, not witches in need of a doctor. The Florest of Ronkledongding is not a place for witches. It is not a place for sick witches. It is not a place where witch doctors are busy.

Standor became a witch doctor because he wanted to have more time to tell stories and more time to practice his favorite medicine. Standor much prefers to cure children than to treat old mean witches that were not around.

Standor is very small. He is even smaller than most Ronkians. Small is a handy thing to be because he also specializes in curing feet and twisted knees. But Standor really prefers to cure children. Because he is small, he can look at them straight in the eye. Then, he winks his wrinkly eyes that have seen rainbows and stars. If the child is really a child, he can see the rainbows and the stars deep inside Standor's eyes. That makes the child smile. A smiling child does not stay sick very long. That is how Standor became known as the favorite doctor for children. The problem is to find Standor because he is a Ronkian. Ronkians are seldom seen. But Coral and Emorix have found him. They are not sick, but they found him just the same, and he makes them smile.

Not many people have heard of the Ronkians. Fewer have seen them. Only a handful has heard them speak. Fewer than a footful have really understood what they said.

The Ronkians are seldom seen for three reasons:

One, because the Ronkians live upside down at the bottom of the world in the Florest of Ronkledongding. People who live upside up have trouble seeing those who live upside down. They hardly speak to them and never take the time to understand them. Upside Uppers are afraid that if they try to deal with Upside Downers, they will have a pain in the neck.

The second reason why Ronkians are seldom seen is because they come out of the Florest of Ronkledongding only at night. They come out only on dark moonless nights when there is a lot of fog. Even then, they sneak around in the dense fog and in the shadows that would be there if shadows dared going out on such a foggy and dark scary night.

The last reason is the best reason of all. It's the one that is not known. It is the secret reason. Perhaps it is magic. Perhaps it is super magic. Perhaps it is something else. It is a secret that has worked for a very, very long time. So long, that it probably began before "ago" and may last longer than "until". It is such a well-kept secret that even I don't know it. I also expect that you will never find out what the third reason is.

Standor took an immediate liking to the children. They had a very strange adventure that would have scared many grown-ups. Yet, they had not cried. They had kept calm and cool. He was sure they would become good friends. He knew he would help them.

He also liked having new visitors. They have so many interesting things to talk about what they have seen. But what he liked the best was that this was the first time someone from the upside up part of the world was looking at him face to face. The upside uppers have an annoying tendency to stare at the Ronkian people face to feet. Worse, sometimes they just ignore them. Standor found this awkward and annoying. It hurts your neck to always talk to people who are face to feet with you. It is even worse to be ignored - to have people who are close to you and who do not pay attention to your presence. They act as if you are not there. But, because the children had been turned head over heel when they tripped on the edge of the blue band of the rainbow, they were the same side up as Standor was. It is much easier to talk to someone face to face than to talk to them face to feet. That way you can see the answer in their eyes. Standor, who is old and wise, as we already know, found that many times, the answer in someone's eyes is a better answer than the one from someone's mouth.

Standor was very happy with his new visitors.

Standor said: "I will help you, but right now I have to go. I have to make a sick child smile. I am also a doctor".

Coral and Emorix were disappointed that Standor had to go. But they knew that making a sick child smile was of great importance. They understood, but they wished that Standor could stay with them. They were a little bit very much afraid of being left alone in the florest. By then they knew that it was a marvelous place, better, a marlavous place like Standor had said. But it was also a strange place.

It is natural to be afraid of strangeness. Sometimes, when people see strange things, they are more afraid of the "strange" than of the "thing". Standor, who was as wise as he was old, understood the children's feelings. He told them not to worry; he would meet with them as soon as he could. He would meet them right after making the sick child smile. He suggested that the children would like to go to his house and meet his wife. Standor's wife is a scientist. She likes receiving visitors.

He explained that the house was easy to find. All the children had to do was to go towards the Rainbow Falls, past the big rock that won't do a thing. Then they should trace their steps back to the big rock. At the big rock, they should turn towards the potrose garden, take a deep breath to smell the perfume from the flowers and then go back four hundred and twenty paces. That would put them close to the biggest dizzy. At the biggest dizzy, they were to turn around once and then go straight until they came to a small pond. On the shore of the small pond, they would smell a house of petals from the potroses. This is where Standor said he lived. They had to be careful not to touch the big potrose thorns that were on the outside of the hut. They were to knock on the door. Standor's wife, the scientist works at home. She would be glad to welcome the children. They could have a bite to eat and rest until Standor could come and meet with them again.

Coral was very good at making maps. She made maps for her father every evening so that he could find his way to their bed and tuck them in. There were many times when the father had not read the map very well. He had lost his way to the children's bed. Once the father tried to tuck-in the closet. Another time he kissed the doorknob good night. One night he even pulled the window curtains way up to the dresser's chin as if it were a blanket.

Coral had made a very good map. She had written the directions down very carefully. She was scratching her head. She looked puzzled when she asked: "why would we go to the big rock and then to the Rainbow Falls and then back to the big rock? Is that not wasting our time?"

Standor looked surprised at the question. "Certainly" he said "you would not want to be so near the Rainbow Falls as you will be when you are at the big rock, without taking a few extra steps to go and see the fall? That cannot be a waste of time! The Rainbow Falls is so pretty! The children nodded. They understood.

Standor was pleased that they did. With a bright smile that looked like a wink and a song, he left them. He went to cure the child.

The Kangadrool and the Crocrosmile

Coral and Emorix started walking carefully along the path that Standor had shown them.

At first, they were silent and careful. They looked at all the new and wondricus things around them. They had never seen flowers so big. They had never smelled flowers so sweet smelling. They also liked looking at all the birds living in the flowers. They wondered if they would find their friend, the one-legged bird who was sorry he had only five wings. There were many birds - some had as much as nine wings. They did not fly like the birds they had seen near their house. They sort of bopped and flupted. Some were going forward. Others were going backward, but most of them were going sideways. One very pretty purple bird with green teeth was flying upside down. Another one, a pink bird that looked like cotton candy was not flying at all. He floated up in the air just like a kite.

The longer they walked the more relaxed and happier they became. They were very relaxed and very happy until they heard a loud thump and another loud thump coming their way from further down the path. They cringed and decided to hide behind the roots of a truelip. The thumps were coming closer. The thumps were louder. The thumps were faster. Thump! Thump thump!

The children were not sure if it was the thumps that were making the earth shake or whether it was, they who were shaking from the worst fear they ever had.

They remembered being scared when their father told them the story of the "ghost who would return" or the story of the "ghost who would return again", or worse than worse, the story of the "ghost who would not return again because it was too scary to return".

They remembered being scared when they had heard the sound of the wolves when their parents took them camping at the lake during their holidays last year.

They remembered being scared when they heard their father scream in pain in the middle of the night last month. That fear had stopped only when they found out he was not under attack by a burglar. He had bumped his big toe on the table leg as he was going to get a glass of water in the dark.

They remembered all these scary things. But they could not remember being as scared as they were now. The thumps and the other thumps were getting closer and closer to where they were. They were scared. They were terrified.

They clung as low to the ground as they could. Of course, the closer they were to the ground, the louder the thump became and the more they could feel the ground shaking.

Thump! Thump! Not more than 150 paces away.

Thump! Thump! Thump! Not more than 100 paces away

Thump! Thump! Thump! Thump! Not more than 50 paces away.

Thump! Thump! Thump! Thump! Thump! Closer and closer, each thump was getting closer. Then, very near, just on the other side of the truelip roots. Thump! And then - worse! - No more thump!

The children were hiding, but deep down inside their heart they knew that the thumps had stopped because they had been seen. What was going to happen to them?

Then they heard it, the big deep voice.

"Who are you? Why are you in my way? Who are you hiding from?

Then the big deep voice asked trembling "Should I be hiding with you?" Is it dangerous?"

Emorix slowly looked up. He was the first to see it.

Then Coral saw it.

They both saw it.

They also saw that it was seeing them.

There it was. The nicest smile they had ever seen on a Kangaroo.

"Hi, I am a kangadrool. Are you kangadrools too?"

"Do you know how to speak?" He asked with his very deep and slurpitty, spluttery voice.

The kangadrool was so proud that he had learned to speak that he asked everyone he met whether they could speak.

"No, we are not kangaroos and yes, of course we know how to speak!" said Emorix. "But this is the first time we speak to a kangaroo."

"A kangaroo? What is a kangaroo? Are they dangerous? Should I hide?"

The children were about to say: "You are a kangaroo." Then, they remembered how things in the Florest of Ronkledongding had strange names.

They said: "Never mind, you don't have to hide." We are Coral and Emorix. "Could you please tell us who you are again?"

"I am a kangadrool. It is very nice to meet you." The kangadrool had learned to be polite from his mother. "Tell me should I also be afraid? Is there a scary thing about to happen?"

The children laughed and told him that they had been afraid of his thumps and were hiding from him. The kangarool started shaking from laughter.

It is dangerous when the belly of a kangadrool shakes with laughter when his pouch is full of water.

The kangadrool found the thought that the children were hiding from him to be a very funny joke. He started to laugh. He laughed louder. Then he laughed louder than loud.

He was laughing so much that his belly that was full of water wiggled, gurgled and giggled.

For every ha ha there would be a gurgle and another gurgle and another gurgle. For every hee hee there would be a splash and another splash. Then the Kangadrool did what a kangadrool with a pouch full of water should never do.

He laughed so much that he slapped his belly!

Water! Water! There was water everywhere and too many drops to drink.

This is what happened. The water from the pouch had splashed when the kangadrool slapped his belly. The children, the kangadrool and the truelip roots were soaked. They were soaked to the roots.

They took a deep breath. They shook the water from their hair. They shook the water from their eyes. They shook the water from the tip of their noses. Everyone shook the water from the tip of his nose except the truelips. Truelips do not have tips on their noses – they do not even have noses.

The children and the Kangadrool looked at each other again. They started to laugh again. It was a great belly laugh. Here I have to be precise. The great belly laugh was not an ordinary laugh from a great belly. It was a great laugh from a normal belly. It was a great belly laugh. One that could have been heard from very far away had it not been drowned by an even bigger and deeper throat laugh from directly behind the children and almost beside the kangadrool.

Who could have a bigger and deeper throat laugh than the sound made from the laughter made by two children and one kangadrool laughing as hard as they could?

No one except...

Yes - that.

The children were staring at one thousand and many more teeth. Past the teeth they were staring at a red and pointed tongue. Past the tongue there was a cavernous throat. They could see past a huge set of tonsils. They could see all the way into a huge belly. The belly was empty. They could see so far inside the tummy that had that huge mouth swallowed Jonah - the children could have seen Jonah. And, if Jonah had been reading a book, and if the children had a flashlight, they could have read the book with him. Now they could see straight down all the way to the inside of the tip of a long tail. Never, had the children seen such a large mouth! They were also very happy to notice that there were no children inside the stomach. But there certainly was room for some - at least two!

The laughter was deep, but it was not a mean, wicked witch of the center, (she is meaner that the wicked witch of the North) type of laugh. It was a happy and throaty laugh. It was the laugh of a crocosmile.

His laugh made the children laugh harder. The children's harder laugh made the kangadrool laugh even harder. The kangadrool's even louder laugh made the crocosmile laugh much harder than all of them laughing together!

When he was laughing, the crocosmile was banging his tail on the ground. When he was laughing, the kangadrool was hopping up and down. I was like a dance. Slam would go the tail. Hop would go the feet. Slam! Hop! Slam! Hop! Then thump…

Yes, the hopping feet had landed on the slammed tail. The tail owner stopped laughing. He did not like his tail to be hopped on. The feet owner stopped laughing. He did not like hopping on tails. He did not like hurting someone who had such a fun laugh as a crocosmile! Also, he did not think that it was a good idea to hop on the tail of someone who had such a big mouth and so many teeth - just in case!

The children stopped laughing because the others had stopped laughing. They felt sad for the crocosmile whose tail might hurt.

The Children, the Kangadrool and the Crocosmile are having a big laugh party. Would you like to join them?

They felt sad for the kangadrool who visibly felt sad because he may have hurt his friend.

"Are you hurt?" said the kangadrool to the crocosmile?

"Not very much" said the crocosmile who had recovered his smile. Our tails are so long that it takes a long time for the pain to reach our brains. By the time the pain gets to our brains, we forget what the pain was about. Many times, it is not what hurt you, it is who hurt you and how you were hurt that hurts the most, not the pain itself. The pain is often only a small part of the hurt. Not remembering what hurt you often reduces the hurt.

At least this is the way crocosmiles think. That is what we learn in Crocosmile School. Not being able to remember the cause of the hurt is probably why we always look so happy."

It was actually a good thing that the kangadrool's stomp landed on the crocosmile's tail. No one could have laughed as hard as they had been laughing much longer.

The Crocosmile's Watch

"Hello, I am Coral and this is my brother Emorix".

"Pleased to meet you" smiled the crocosmile who had learned to be polite from his mother. Crocosmiles, do not say their words, they smile them. I think this is a good idea. I think that people should also smile the words that they want to say. Not a "big bad wolf, better to see you with my dear" kind of smile. Not a "wait until I get my hands on you" kind of mean smile. No, it was just a big happy and friendly kind of smile, like the smile of the crocosmile. If people smiled like that when they speak, there would be fewer people who are sad because of what they hear. There might even be fewer people who are sad because of what they say.

Like the crocosmile whose tail was so long that he could not remember what caused the pain by the time the pain reached his brain. Maybe we have spent so much time with the laughing story that you forgot that Coral and Emorix had just left Standor and were on their way to meet his wife at their house by way of the Rainbow Falls.

The conversation with the crocosmile continued.
.

"I have never seen you here before," smiled the crocrosmile. "Was I looking the wrong way?"

"No," said Emorix. "We just slid down the rainbow a few minutes ago."

"Gee, I hope you went down the blue stripe, it is my favorite, it is so fast" said the kangadrool.

"it is a good thing you came this way. If you had gone to the other end of the rainbow, you would have a pot of gold instead of the barrel of laughs we just had". I do not know why some people put laughs inside a barrel, but it seems to work.

"Gold is nice," said Coral.

"Yes, I guess so, but it does not make you laugh as much as we did a minute ago."

"Some people think gold makes you happy," said Emorix who never had gold before. He did not know for sure.

"You are right. I think it may even be true. Can it make you as happy as when you eat a sweet honey sandwich made by the monkbees? Can it make you as happy as when you see the Rainbow Falls, or smell the lolly of the volley? Can it make you as happy as Standor is happy when he sees a sick child smile? I am not sure that it can." said the kangadrool.

"Gold may be nice - but the florest is pretty. It is nice and it is here. I like being here because my friends are here," said the crocosmile.

Coral said, "I think you are right. It is a bit like us. We would give up the pot of gold to be with our friends and to be with our parents. We would be so happy to be with them again. But, tell me kangadrool. Why were you carrying water in your pouch?"

"Ha, it is my job. I help the beleaver with his dam. He has no water. I take the water to him. He needs water to have a dam."

Coral and Emorix were not quite sure they understood. They were about to ask about it when the kangadrool said: "I forgot! I must go! I am late! I must take more water to the beleaver!

Goodbye! I am glad to have met you. I would like to be your friend. See you later!"

Hop, hop, the kangadrool bounced away.

The children shouted: "Goodbye. We too would like to be your friends."

"See you again" smiled the crocosmile.

"Where are you going?" He smiled to the children.

"We are going to Standor's house - is it far?"

"Nothing is very far when you can smell the flowers along the way. I forgot to ask. Do you know how to smell?" he grinned.

"Yes," smiled Emorix. "We know how to smell."

"We crocosmiles are very good at smelling." He said as he curled his tail above his head and pointed at his nose.

"This long snout is not only good to smile. It can sniff very well. Some of us have noses that are extra long. If we could bend our snout upward and turn our nostrils out and around, we could smell upwind even when we are downwind."

It took the children some time to imagine what the crocosmile would look like if he tried to do that. The closer they came to forming a picture of a periscopic crocosmile the more they smiled. They had to stop trying to imagine the picture before they had finished. They were afraid to start laughing uncontrollably again.

"There are two ways to get to Standor's house," said the crocosmile. "There is the way that is too quick and there is the very long way. There is also the wrong way, but that does not count."

"Why would anyone go the very long way?" Said Coral.

"There could be lots of reasons," grinned the crocosmile.

"I get it," said Coral. "We may want to choose the very long way so we can see more pretty things like the Rainbow Falls. So we can smell pretty things like the flowers and meet new friends. Is that why we would choose to go the very long way?"

"Now, now, now," smiled the crocosmile. "Tell me. How could you find the way that lets you do all those wonderful things to be very long? Enjoyable things are never long enough. The way of pretty things, new friends, new learning and nice smells is always too short and too quick no matter how much time it takes. It is the way that does not do these things that can be very long, no matter how little time it takes. The way to Standor's house that lets you smell flowers, see pretty things and make new friends is the way that is too quick. Think of times that were nice. Were they long? Time can be measured. But time must also be enjoyed.

"Look at my watch. It has a smile string and a frown string. The smile string slows the watch down. The frown string speeds it up."

The children looked at the crocosmile's watch. It was an hourglass that was strapped to the tip of his tail. The neck of the hourglass was made of rubber. Just like the crocosmile had said - there were two strings around the neck of the hourglass. There was a gold string that could narrow the hole so that the sand flowed through much slower. There was a red string that pulled the hole wide open, so the sand poured through very quickly.

"I pull the gold string when I am happy. The sands of time go slower through the hole. I pull the red string when I am sad. The sands of time go through the hole very fast. The watch is also waterproof," grinned the crocosmile. "I would not want time to stop when I am crying or when it is raining."

"Does it work? Does it really slow down and speed up time?" Said Emorix.

"I don't think it really does. But it is nice to think that it does. Sometimes pulling the red string is enough to make me think that it is time to stop being sad."

Suddenly Coral had her 'I think I know how to play this game' look. The same look she has when she gets in arguments with her father. Arguments about whether airplanes taking off at the bottom of the world are going up or whether they have to go down to get away from the earth. At first, she had been very serious about the discussion. She thought that her job was to make sure that her dad understood what was right. Later... that's when the spark in her smile first appeared - she realized that the game of matching wits was a lot more fun than trying to make her daddy right. It was also much easier. Sometimes the game you play is more important than the results of that game. That is not to say that Coral did not always care if she was winning or losing. She cared very much. She liked to win.

"I see." She said. "And… what is the wrong way?"

"Ha!" Smiled the crocosmile. "The wrong way is not the right way."

"Ha!" Coral said. "Why is that?"

It now was time for the crocosmile to put on his world famous 'I think I fooled her look.'

"Because the wrong way does not get there," He was very pleased that he had tricked her. He started giggling and giggling and giggling, again and again and again. The giggles grew into guffaws. The guffaws became laughs. The laughs became uncontrolled. The laugh went from his throat. It vibrated trough the length of his body. It made his tail wiggle and flap. If the crocosmile had long pointed ears they would have fallen three inches down to the edge of his chin. It is a good thing that crocosmiles do not have long pointed ears.

"But," said Coral, "what if the wrong way got to a better place - a place that had many more friends, many more flowers and many more birds. Would that not make it the right way?"

The crocosmile stopped laughing. He stopped wiggling. He even stopped smiling. A worried frown appeared in his face. He, who was pretty good at explaining how things really should be and how things are, had met another who was very good at it. It was almost as if these children had always lived in the florest. They understood the way to speak.

Suddenly the crocosmile had a brilliant idea. He would make them his children. He would adopt them. He would teach them how to be crocosmiles. His heart grew very warm at the thought of having Coral and Emorix as his crocosmile children. He would have two of the smartest and most polite little crocosmiles at Crocrosmile School. He would be so proud of that. Of course, he would have to teach them how to smile wider and how to walk lower. That would not be too hard. What a great idea!

He was so excited he stammered as he smiled his words.

"WWWWWait. I I I I have a great idea. Will you two become my children? I will take good care of you."

That surprised the children. They liked the crocosmile. They were flattered that he wanted to adopt them. Adopted children are special. The children felt they were chosen. But they still wanted to remain their parents' children. They had to think hard to find a way to say no. To find a way that would not hurt the crocosmile.

"We already have parents," said Emorix. "We love them very much. They love us very much. They take good care of us. We would like to go back to them some day soon. We like it here. We like you very much. But, at the end of our adventure we will want to go back to our home and be with our parents."

Now they knew what the crocosmile must have looked like when he was still a crocogrump - or at least when he was a crocomope.

Both children were deeply touched by his sadness. Thank goodness that Emorix had another of his good plans. He said: "We had so much fun with you today. You also told us so many wise and good things. We would like to make you our partner."

"Yes," said Coral. "You can be our very special partner. Partners are not exactly like parents, but they are very close friends who can help us. Yes, we would very much like you to be our partner."

The smile was shaky at first. The eyes peered up. The lips started to quiver a little bit. Slowly the shape of the crocosmile's mouth changed from the droopy banana of a mope to the rainbow of a happy smile. Don't forget that the crocosmile, like everything else in the florest, was upside down. That is why his mouth had the shape of a rainbow when he smiled. Then the smile moved upwards towards the eyes. The eyes are where a smile truly lives.

"It is good that I can be your special partner. But on one condition, you have to be my special partners too."

"Of course, we'll be your special partners," said Emorix.

"Great, lets shake paws on that." Smiled the crocosmile. Each child had two hands. The crocrosmile had four paws. He turned over on his back. He raised all four of his paws. The children each shook two paws. It was exiting, they had never shaken a crocosmile's paws before. Come to think of it they had never shaken a real crocodile's paws either.

The crocosmile was very happy to be the children's special partner. The children were also very happy. They were happier than they thought they would be. The crocosmile was also their first real special partner. It felt good to have a partner.

"Now we have to go to Standor's house. Will you come with us?" Said Coral.

"I like Standor. He is good and wise. He is a good police officer, and he is a good doctor also. You are lucky to have him as a friend. He is my friend too, but he is not my partner. I am sorry. I cannot go with you. But partners, I will let Standor know where I will be. If you need your special partner, just call me. Meanwhile let me give you my watch. It is always good to know what time it is. Also remember the secret of the watch. If the red cord is pulled when you are sad, the sands of time flow faster. You are not sad for long. If the gold cord is pulled when you are happy, they flow slower. You are happy longer."

The playful smile had come back to the crocosmile face. His eyes were full of the smile. Just like before, the children recognized his way of thinking in what he had said. They were very glad to take the watch. Emorix thanked him. He looked at the watch and smiled. Emorix put the watch around his wrist. "You are a real friend and a good special partner."

Saying their goodbye, the children started walking away towards the big rock. Quite often they looked back and waved. They kept doing that until they could no longer see the waving tail of their new partner.

The Great Big Rock

The crocosmile had been right. The children were seeing many new wondricus and marlavous things along the path. Everything smelled so delicious. The sounds they heard made them want to dance, sing, smile and whistle. The sounds were like the sounds of a magical flute. The sound the flute would make, if a very happy magical flute player played it. The colors were just as bright as the eyes of a puppy when you come back home to him. The temperature was warm, but not too hot. Coral was enjoying herself very much. She told Emorix to pull the gold rope on the crocosmile's watch. She did not want the time to go too fast. But she spoke too late.

Emorix was feeling as happy as his sister was. He had already pulled twice on the gold cord.

Then it happened. They heard a clop and a flop. It was a light sound at first. There was a bit of a clop and a bit of a flop. First the clop grew louder. After that, the flop grew much louder. It became a clearer bit of a clop and a clearer bit of a flop. Then again louder - a bigger bit of a clop and a bigger bit of a flop. Could it be that danger was lurking in such a wondricus place as the Florest of Ronkledongding? Maybe yes - maybe no.

Before the clops and the flops could grow much louder - the children saw what made those sounds. It was coming in their direction. It was coming nearer. The nearer it came, the bigger it got. It had a bright yellow head with only one hair on it. Can something be scarier that a yellow headed thing with only one hair on it?

They saw that the clops and the flops sounds were made by the biggest, blackest feet that something with a yellow head with only one hair on it could have at the end of their legs. Could that be the answer? Could it be that what was scarier than a yellow head with only one hair on it, was a yellow head with one hair on it with clopping and flopping enormously enormous black feet? It could be.

The children took a deep breath. They wondered what to do. Then they heard it. It was whistling happily like a bird. Something that whistles as happily as a bird cannot be as mean as one would think a yellow head with only one hair on it would possibly be.

As it was getting nearer, the children could see that it was a man. He did not have a yellow head. He wore a yellow safety plastic hat on his head. He had a pair of big black safety boots on his feet. There was a single feather on top of the hat. He had a silly smile on his face. His eyes were rolling around. He was spending most of the time looking at the clouds. He looked like a happy man. But he also looked like a very distracted man.

"Hello! I am Emorix and this is my sister Coral. How are you?"

"Have you seen her?" Said the yellow plastic hat man.

"Seen who?" Said Coral.

"Her of my life – my girlfriend," said the man.

"We have not seen anyone lately except the crocosmile and the kangadrool," said Emorix.

"She is not anyone. She is not a crocosmile. She is not a kangadrool. She is "She"." Said the man.

"And who is she?" Said Coral, who thought the man was a bit silly.

"She is the prettiest, most wonderful, best smelling, nicest angel with the prettiest hair in the world. Have you seen her? I call her Ma Reine. It is French you know. It means my queen." Said the man.

He seemed very proud of having said that. He was also proud of being able to speak in French.

Everything he said sounded a little silly to the children.

"Are you in love?" Said Coral. She had guessed.

"Yes," said the man. "I am in love with her. Who would not be? Have you seen her?"

"No, we have not. We have just arrived in the florest. We are on our way to Standor's house," said Emorix.

It was as if the man had not heard them. He looked very distracted. His head was in the clouds and his heart was in his head. That would put his heart in the clouds too. There was not much room left for anything else inside that head. There was not very much room for anything else inside that cloud.

"Where are you going?" Said Coral.

"I am going to meet with her," said the lover.

"Well! Have a good day and good luck to you," said Emorix who had recognized that there was not very much point to try to talk to the lover. He was too much in love to pay attention to anyone or to anything.

"Yes...Yes...goodbye." Giggled the lover as he skipped and hopped away. It looked as if he was trying to breathe in the clouds. Perhaps he was. Just as he disappeared at the end of the path, he stopped. He yelled back. "You are new here. I should warn you. Be careful of the monkbees. Don't stand under the dizzies unless you wear a yellow hat like I do."

The children were happy for him. He looked so happy. He was so much in love. They looked as he skipped further and further away. The bouncing blob of yellow disappeared over the horizon. They were also worried about his warning. They did not understand what it meant. They could not ask him. He was already gone. They would ask their partner, the crocosmile, when they saw him next.

They smiled at each other and continued on their way towards the big rock.

They could see the big rock was not too far away. It was in the middle of the ferns. It was big and brown. They continued walking. Emorix was tempted to pull on the red cord of the crocosmile's watch. He wanted to get there faster. He had second thoughts about pulling on the red cord when he first spotted the monkbees swinging from flower to flower.

"Loo," he said to Coral. "Are these monkeys?"

Coral had already noticed them.

"Yes, I see them. I was about to ask you if they were bees?"

"You are right. They look like bees. But they also look like monkeys. Sometimes they swing from the flowers. Other times they appear to fly. They are strange but they look like fun."

"Hear them buzz and squeal at the same time. What strange animals! Perhaps they are not strange animals. Perhaps they are strange insects," said Coral.

"Nobody will believe us when we go back to school and tell them about this place," said Emorix. Maybe we should bring one to "Show and Tell".

"Watch out! One tossed a coconut our way!" warned Coral.

"It looks like a coconut, but it is much bigger. Let's look at it," said Emorix.

"Be careful, they may throw another one down at us," said Coral.

"Maybe this is what the lover was warning us about."

"Yes, it could be. You keep a look out and warn me if they throw another one," yelled Emorix as he dashed towards the coconut. It was lying there on the path. He ran as fast as he could.

"Careful! Here comes another one," screamed Coral. Emorix easily avoided the second coconut.

"Are they aiming at me?" asked Emorix.

"It looks like it. They think it is some sort of a game. You look safe to me now. They do not have any coconuts in their hands at this moment," hollered Coral above the squeals of the monkbees.

Emorix dashed forward again. He grabbed the coconut in his arms. He was able to return safely to Coral's place before the bees that looked and behaved like monkeys could get another coconut and throw it at him.

The children looked around very carefully. They wanted to find a place where they could not be hit by another coconut. The big rock was only a little bit further ahead. It looked like it would be the safest place to be. Emorix pointed to it. Coral understood right away. Emorix said: "Let's go!". They both ran as fast as they could towards the big rock.

There was a lot of buzzing and shrieking from the top of the flowers. But no one threw any more coconuts at them. They reached the rock. They selected a place that offered all the protection they needed. They looked closely at the coconut.

It was bigger than a normal coconut. There were other differences. Coconuts have hair. This one had a wig. Once the children removed the wig, they found that this coconut had smooth bright red skin. An ordinary coconut has two dark spots that look like eyes. This one had two dark spots that looked like nostrils. It also had a bump that looked like a nose. There were two smaller bumps that looked like ears. There was another bump that looked exactly like another bump. The children found that strange and curious. They had this fruit that looked like a coconut but that did not look very much like a coconut. They had never seen anything like this before.

"This looks strange." Said Coral.

"I wonder what's inside." Emorix took a closer look at the coconut as he said that. He noticed that the shell had cracked - probably from the fall. He forced the coconut open.

The inside of the coconut was like something they had never seen before. A coconut has solid white flesh and milk. This coconut had a bright red inside just like a watermelon. There were also as many pits as there was in a watermelon. Instead of milk like in an ordinary coconut there was a very pretty pink liquid. On top of that there was a very sweet and refreshing smell coming out of the coconut.

"I wonder what it tastes like," said Coral. Emorix took one half of the coconut. He dipped a finger in the pink liquid. He slowly brought the finger to his mouth and licked it. "It is sweet pink lemonade," said Emorix. "It is even cool as if it had just come out of the refrigerator. Here, taste," he said it as he handed her the other half.

Coral had a sip and smacked her lips at the sweet cool taste of the lemonade. She then took a small bite into the red flesh of the coconut. It was also refreshing. "Gee! This part tastes like strawberry and ice cream. That is really good."

Emorix said: "Taste the pits. They are chocolate buds. They taste very good. It is a good thing that we have the coconut. I was getting hungry." Both children ate their half piece of the wonderful fruit that looked a bit like a coconut. The more they ate, the more they liked it. The more they liked it, the more they thought that this was a very wonderful place.

The Antsniffer

Once they had finished eating, Coral said: "Let's check this big rock. There are so many strange things in this florest. For all we know, this rock may be alive. It may even sing."

They spoke to the rock. They poked at the rock. They joked with the rock. They stroked the rock. They choked the rock. They woke the rock! That is what they thought they had done when they heard a yawn. But it was not so. The yawn came from a very bored looking kind of anteater. "What are you doing?" he asked.

"We are trying to see whether the rock is alive," replied the children. They were a little embarrassed at being caught doing something that may be as silly as trying to poke or choke a rock. "Why would anyone want to do a silly thing like that?" asked the anteater.

"Hello, I am Emorix, this is my sister Coral, may we ask who you are?"

"Hello, I am Andy the ant sniffer. I am pleased to meet you. Now let me be a little more precise than that. My identity is not pleased to meet you. My identity is Andy. Andy is my name. Ant sniffing is my game. Pleased, is my reaction at meeting you. Now, is that clear? Clarity is important you know. Now please tell me clearly. Why were you doing what you were doing?"

The Antsniffer sniffs ants.
Is that gross?

"There are so many strange things in this florest. We thought that the rock might also be strange. We decided to see whether it was alive."

"Why would a rock be alive? Rocks do not live. It is not very clear to me why you would think that a rock would be alive. I do not think that you are thinking very clearly. Let me be more precise. I did not mean to say that I do not think. I think. What I think is that you are not thinking very clearly," said the ant sniffer.

"I know that we looked silly," said Emorix softly, "Since we have arrived here, we have seen so many unusual things that we thought that the rock might also be unusual. We thought that it could be a special rock. One like we have never seen before."

"You must be much clearer than that. Let me help you. What did you mean when you said "since we have arrived"?" asked the ant sniffer.

"We came to the florest just this morning. We live very far away from here," said Coral.

"Ha, you are tourists. Where is your camera? Tourists always carry cameras strapped around their necks. I don't see you carrying a camera. Perhaps you are not what you say you are," said the ant sniffer suspiciously.

"We are not tourists. We did not say we were. We came here by accident," explained Emorix.

"Ah, an accident, did you get hurt?" asked the ant sniffer who looked concerned.

"No," said Coral, who saw that this conversation was going to last very long. But it would not get anywhere. Yet despite his annoying need to clarify everything, she liked the ant sniffer. She continued being very careful with each of her words. We did not have the type of accident that causes injuries. What we meant to say is that we left our home accidentally. It was not our intention to leave our home. We did not mean to leave our home at all. It happened as a result of an unplanned event. After we left the area where we live - we drifted away from our home until we came across the rainbow. We slid down the blue band of the rainbow and landed in the florest.

"Ah, you came by rainbow. That makes everything clear to me." Said the ant sniffer as if he met rainbow travelers every day. It is much better to travel by rainbow that by moonbeams. I find the moonbeams are too bumpy. Don't you think so?" asked the ant sniffer.

"I do not know. I have never been on a moonbeam before," said Emorix.

Emorix thought it was odd that simple statements were unclear. But the strange explanation that Coral had given was taken as if it was clear and normal. It was taken as if it did not require further explanations. It was strange, but it was not unpleasant. Somehow it fitted with everything they had encountered up to that time. "Tell me." He said, "I have never seen an ant sniffer, what do you do?"

"Let me be clear about what I do. I sniff ants with my nose."

"That is clear. How do you do it?" asked Coral.

"Let me be precise. I sneak quietly on the tip of my toes until I get close to an ant. Then I sniff the ant."

"Why do you do that? asked Emorix.

"Let me answer clearly. I sniff ants because I am an ant sniffer."

Emorix could see great possibilities in that conversation. A spark of mischief glittered in his eyes when he asked: "Why are you an ant sniffer?"

"Ah! That should be clear to anyone. I am an ant sniffer because I sniff ants."

Emorix said: "Let me see whether I understood you clearly. You sniff ants because you are an antsniffer and you are an antsniffer because you sniff ants. Did I understand you clearly?"

"Yes, you did," said the ant sniffer.

"I have never heard of ant sniffers before," said Emorix. "I have only heard of ant eaters. Do you eat ants?"

"Eat ants. No - I do not eat ants." replied the ant sniffer haughtily. "That would be unhygienic, disgusting and gross - yuck!"

"I understand what you have said...clearly," said Coral. "Thank you very much. Are we to understand that there is nothing special about this big rock? That it is just like all the other rocks we have seen"

"Tell me," said the ant sniffer. "Which rock are you speaking of? Be clear please."

"This rock that I am touching," said Coral with a smile as she placed her hand on the great big rock.

"Please clarify for me. Is it the rock that you are touching with your left shoe or is it the rock that you are touching with your left hand?"

Coral looked at her foot. Her left shoe was on top of a small pebble. She was frustrated but she was also amused. The obsession with clarity was funny and she had to admit the ant sniffer was right. She was touching two different stones.

"The rock that I am touching with my left hand" said Coral.

"That is clear to me now. It is a wrong understanding to think the rock is not special. There are many special things about this great big rock. Look at its color. Look at its size. Imagine its age. Think of the many minerals that make up the rock. Look at the marks on its surface. Some could be scratches made by glaciers. They tell you much about its history. Look at the moss growing on one side. Look at the many insects that live under it. Of course, there are many things special about this great big rock. It is like the other rocks you have seen only in the sense that they too are unique and reflect a very different history."

The children had not expected this type of answer. They thought about it. It was true there were many things special about the rock.

Emorix was the first to speak. "Thank you. What you said is very good for us. We had not thought of the rock that way."

"Good." Said Coral. "The rock that I am touching with my left hand is special. We thank you for pointing that out to us. Now if you will excuse us, we must go to the Rainbow Falls."

"And I must go and sniff ants. It was nice meeting both of you. Have a good trip to the Rainbow Falls. To go there you should go in that direction." As he said that, the ant sniffer pointed towards one of the many lanes that went around the great big rock."

The children watched as the ant sniffer left in another direction. They were holding a lot of snickers inside their belly and under their breath. They knew it was not polite to laugh in front of him. They also were a little bit afraid. What if he heard them and asked them to explain clearly why they were laughing?

They watched him sniff an ant. The sight was quite amusing. The sniffer approached the ground with its long nose. He then sniffed - tentatively at first and deeper later. Then it appeared as if the large sniff had drawn the ant deep inside the ant sniffer's nostril. Perhaps the ant tickled the inside of the ant sniffer's nose, it made him sneeze very hard. Stattchoooo ... Then, as if it was blown out of a pea shooter, the ant shot out of his nostril faster than it at come in.

As soon as the ant sniffer was clearly beyond hearing range and beyond eyesight range Emorix said: "That was clear." Both children fell to the ground laughing uncontrollably.

"Tell me clearly. Was he an ant sniffer or an ant sneezer?" asked Coral. They laughed again. But they also had to admit that the ant sniffer had said something very wise about the rock. He had pointed that, although it was not doing anything, the great big rock was something very unique. It was very special. In that sense there was something special about everything and everyone. They were glad they were now aware of that.

"Enough about the big rock. Now it is time to go to Rainbow Falls." Said Coral.

On the Way to the Rainbow Falls

The path to the Rainbow Falls was as new and as fascinating as anything the children had seen to date. They marveled at the sights. The stems of the flowers were so big. Some were even bigger than "so big". The colors were very bright. Some were as bright as the stars. Others were brighter than that. Even the sharpest and grooviest coloring crayons could not reproduce those colors. Coral said: "Look up there. Look at the tulips. They are a mix of orange and blue. They are so big."

"Look across the path from them," said Emorix. "Look at the size of this dandelion. Father would get very mad if they grew that big on our lawn. A single one would cover the whole lawn. Dad would have to use his big axe to cut it. It would take him hours. Perhaps it would take him days to do it. I would like to help him."

"Let's walk around the stem of this flower." suggested Coral. "It is so large. It will take us longer than it does to go around our house." They did, and it did. It took many minutes. They counted their paces. It had taken them each 342 normal steps plus 17 giant steps and two leaps to get around the stem of only one flower.

"Imagine how big a vase we would need for a bouquet of flowers like these. Imagine how big the table would have to be to hold the vase. Florist shops would have to be inside big skyscrapers. Their trucks would have to be bigger than trains," exclaimed Emorix.

They kept imagining how things would have to be to accommodate the size of the flowers - if the flowers were used as flowers are used at home. They found that game very amusing.

It was not only the size of the flowers that was fascinating. It was not only the colors. The children mentioned that the smells that came from them were so sweet. They thought that the smells were not too strong, but they were everywhere. One smelled sweet like the taste of a raspberry. That is without the pits getting stuck in your teeth. Another smell was soft like velvet feels. Another was cool like spring water on a hot day. Another smell was warm like a snugly blanket. It was cuddly like flannel bunny pajamas – the kind with feet. One smell was a happy smell. It was happy like Christmas morning is. Another smell was - loving. Loving like a grandmother's arms can be. One smell got into the mind. A bit like a good idea gets into the mind. A smell made you feel good like happy music does. The smells were everywhere and nowhere at the same time. They were there all the time, but they did not force themselves upon you. Somehow, like soft music or like happy music, they affected you even if you did not pay attention to them. The smells did not force you to pay attention to them. But if you paid attention to the smells, they carried you like a magic carpet would carry you across a wonderful world of different and beautiful things.

As they walked towards the Rainbow Falls the children invented a new game. They started playing the smelling game. It is a little bit like looking up at the clouds and challenging the other to see the same shape as you do. Instead, they would sniff something and challenge the other to say what it smelled like.

Emorix started it. He picked a handful of bark chips from the ground and smelled it.

"Look, it smells like a Sunday breakfast on Mother's Day." He said.

Coral agreed but thought it was more like a Father's Day brunch. She picked part of a leaf and put her nose to it.

"Ah, this one smells like passing a test at school." She spoke.

"I think you are right. But it could also be the smell of getting a gold star and an A++ on a difficult homework." They agreed that this was a sweet smell indeed.

"What does this one smell like?" Asked Emorix as he handed a twig to his sister.

"It smells like the end of the school year. Can you smell the freshness of the change? Can you smell the wind of new games and the smile of new friends mixed with the warmth of a sunny summer day?"

"No, I think it smells more like Christmas morning. It smells like excitement, candies, pretty wrappings, love and happiness."

They both laughed. They agreed that whether it was the end of the school year or Christmas morning. It was a happy holiday type of a smell.

"And these?" Coral said as she handed a handful of seeds to Emorix?

"Wow! I never smelled anything like this. It is as if all the candies and all the fruits and all the sugar in the world were in the same smell. It is the smell of a smile and of laughter."

Coral said: "I think it is the smell of home and of our parents. It is the smell of happiness and comfort."

Suddenly the children looked at each other. It was happening to them. They were talking and thinking like those who lived in the florest. Before their arrival they would have spoken of the smell of chocolate, of freshly baked bread and the smell of French fries - not the smell of a smile or the smell of a nice dream. The ways of the creatures of the Florest of Ronkledongding was catching up to them. They talked about that.

They did not mind what was happening to their way of thinking and to their way of saying things. However, they agreed that at all time they must remain conscious of the change. They should also be able to talk and think the way they used to think and talk.

They decided to go further forward along the path. They liked to listen to the different sounds in the florest. They wondered whether the smell game could also be played with the sounds.

"Listen to that bird." Said Coral. "It sounds like a sunny winter day."

"Yes," Said Emorix, "and the sound of the wind through the flowers sounds like thinking about our grandmother."

They went on and played some more as they advanced further forward on the way to the Rainbow Falls. Time was passing very fast. It was as if Emorix had forgotten to pull on the gold cord from the crocosmile's watch. Yet, Emorix had pulled on that cord many times. I guess that they were enjoying themselves so much that even slow time looked like it was passing much too fast.

The Nasty Tertiums

For the first time they noticed that the pathway felt very different. It was not like walking on a normal path or like walking on a sidewalk. It was a lot softer. There was a lot more spring in their steps. They had walked for a long time, but their feet and their legs were not tired. That was another thing special about the florest. The paths were made in a way that walking, running, or skipping on them was not tiring. They were talking about that when they hear a loud whisper. It was a whisper - but it was loud enough for them to hear from where they were.

The whisperer said: "Look at them, they are not very big, but they are pretty."

"Yes, they must be rare. I have never seen anything like the two of them before. Look at the colors. There is yellow, green, blue and red," said a second whispering voice.

"Yes, they will be perfect. They will go well with the others."

"Let's wait until they pass by us. We will pick them. Mother will be so happy."

The children looked everywhere to see who was whispering these words. They looked down the path. They could not see anyone coming. They looked beside the path. They still could not see anybody. The voices seemed to come from much higher above. They peered towards the petals of the flowers. Still, the children could not see anyone who was whispering these words.

Then the children thought about what the voices had said. They had spoken about picking two of them. They said they wore green, red, blue and yellow. They spoke of doing it when they passed them. It was clear to the children. The voices were whispering about picking them up. The children were in danger. What to do?

They had heard the voices planning to wait for them to advance further forward. They decided that for the moment they would wait. They would not advance further forward. They would wait until they found out who was whispering about grabbing them. They would wait until they had a plan to deal with that danger.

They had to be careful to ensure that the voices would not sneak up on them while they were talking.

The children kept silent. They listened carefully for any clue as to where the danger was coming from. Emorix even thought of putting his ear to the ground in case the whispering creature would move forward. He was sure that he would hear the sound of their footsteps if they came closer. The children placed themselves in the middle of the path. They chose an area where they could see in all directions quite far away. This way they would be warned ahead of time if the voices tried to rush in and grab them.

The children thought of many different plans.

They thought of calling their partner the crocosmile. He would know what to do. He might be able to help them. Unfortunately, they did not know where the crocosmile was. They did not know how to call him.

They also thought of turning around and going directly to Standor's house. He would know what to do. But Standor had been very keen about them going to Rainbow Falls. They felt they should go. They did not want to disappoint him. Also, after the many strange and marlavous things they had seen so far, the children were very curious about the Rainbow Falls. Everyone they had met had commented on how special it was. For something to be considered special in a place where already there are so many very special things – that something must be extra special. It might even be extra very special. The children were quite excited about seeing the Rainbow Falls.

They also thought of going back to the big rock. They could try to find a different road to the Rainbow Falls. Find a road that would avoid this part of the florest. The problem with that idea was that they did not know which of the many other paths would be the right path to take. There was too much of a choice. They continued to think about making a plan to avoid the danger. They also continued to watch and listen to make sure the voices were not approaching. Then, they heard the whispers once more.

It said: "They are not advancing. They are staying there. How are we going to pick them if they don't come nearer?"

"I don't know." Said the other whispering voice. "We need them. They have such pretty colors. They are so small. They are so cute. They must also smell pretty."

"I have an idea," said the first whisperer. "I will call them."

"Good idea but be sneaky about it. Make sure you trick them."

The children looked at each other. They were afraid because the whisperers were still planning to catch them. They were also reassured by what they heard. The whisperers did not seem to be able to get close enough to them to be able to grab them from where they were. However, they were very much afraid about hearing that the whisperers found them so small. Whoever they were, they must be very big if they thought the children were very small. The children were also quite a bit amused that the whisperers did not seem to realize that they could hear them and were aware of their plans. It would be difficult to fool the children now that the children were aware that the voices were trying to fool them.

One of the whispering voices called loudly at them. "Hello! Can we be friends? Come and play with us."

"Hello," said Coral. "Who are you"?

"I am Cadwallader. Come and play with me."

"Nice to meet you Cadwallader. Are you alone?"

"No, my sister is with me."

"Good, what is you sister's name?"

"Her name is Balboa."

"That's a nice name," said Coral who always liked the name Balboa.

"Yes, she likes her name very much. Our father chose our names. Come forward so we can hear you better."

"Can't you come here?" said Coral.

"No, we cannot. You will have to come here."

Coral smiled at Emorix. "Why can't you come?" said Coral?

"Because our roots are too deep, and we have no shoes. You come to us. We will have lots of fun."

"Do you have roots?" Said Coral as she was winking at Emorix.

"Of course, we do. Don't you?"

"No, we don't have roots. What kind of game could we play?" asked Emorix.

"We could play pickee pickee."

"What is pickee pickee? Emorix thought the voices could be sneakier than that. "How do you play it?"

"It is a very good game. You come forward to where my sister and I are. We will show you. You will like it."

"We cannot see you. Where are you?" Asked Coral.

"We are just ahead of you, across from the chrisentenmaximums, and just before the red truelip."

"Are you flowers?" Said Coral. "What kind of flower are you?"

"We are flowers. We are the prettiest and sweetest smelling flowers. We are nasty tertiums. Can't you see our pretty orange petals?"

The children saw the nasty tertiums. There were two of them weaving in the wind. They were very big indeed and they were very tall indeed. They were at least seven times as big and seven times as tall as their uncle Richard was, and he is quite tall.

"Yes, we see you now." Said Emorix. "We did not know that flowers knew how to talk."

"Don't be silly," said Balboa. "Of course, we can talk. How else would we be able to sing?"

"We are glad that you can talk and sing. Would you sing a song for us?" asked Emorix.

"Yes, we would like to sing for you. Come nearer to us. You will be able to hear our song better."

"We can hear well from here," said Coral.

"When we sing, people say that they hear us much better when they are closer. We have very soft voices when we sing. Come nearer."

"No, we hear very well. Our friends say we can hear a pin drop. We don't need to come closer to hear you," said Emorix.

"Yes, but you do need to be nearer to play pickee pickee - its so much fun."

"We don't even know how to play pickee pickee. Tell us the rules."

"It is easy," said Cadwallader. "You and Coral come to where we are. That is the first rule."

"What happens after that?" Said Coral

"Lots of fun happens after that," said the biggest nasty tertium.

"What kind of fun?" Asked Coral

"Fun fun," said Balboa. "The best fun of all."

Nasty tertiums invite the children to play the "pickee pickee" game.

They plan to capture the children.

Do you think they should play?

Would you play that game?

"I see. Who has the fun? You, us or all of us?" asked Emorix.

"Lots of fun," replied Balboa, avoiding answering the question.

"Is there something to eat in your game?" said Emorix who wanted to make sure that he and his sister would not become a meal for the nasty tertiums.

"No, not exactly," said Balboa. "Come, we will show you how to play the game."

"Are you hungry?" asked Cadwallader. "If you are, you can come here. We have very good dirt full of iron, potash, nitrogen and calcium. We can share with you."

"We don't eat dirt, even when it is full of iron, potash, nitrogen and calcium. We are not hungry. We ate a very good coconut a little while ago."

"What is a coconut?"

"These are coconuts," said Emorix, pointing to one that was hanging from a pretty purple flower.

"This is not a coconut. It is a choconut," said Balboa.

"We don't have choconuts now. But if you play pickee pickee with us we will give you a choconut as a prize," promised Balboa.

"We will give you two," said Cadwallader.

"We will give you three, said Balboa, who could recognize a good idea when Cadwallader had one.

"We will give you four and thirty-seven thirteen sixty," said Cadwallader who wanted to use as big a number as he could think of. Cadwallader was not very good at thinking of very big numbers.

"That would be nice," Ssid Coral. She thought that it would be a good idea to speak before the nasty tertiums could think of a bigger number.

Coral asked: "Can you bend down and reach all the way to the ground?"

"Yes, we can. We have to do that when we play pickee pickee," replied Balboa.

"Can you show us how you bend down?" said Coral.

"Yes – look," said Balboa. She bent her head down until her petals reached the ground. It was very gracious. For someone who could become one of the "pickee", it was also very threatening and scary.

"That is pretty," said Coral. "Can you do it faster?"

"Yes," said Balboa as she did it faster.

"Great!" said Coral. "Let us see you do it the fastest you can."

"Goody, goody!" said Balboa. "I like doing it the fastest. Watch me". She did it faster than the last time.

"That was very fast. Can Cadwallader do it much faster?" asked Emorix who had caught on to Coral's plan.

"Of course, I can do it faster than Balboa. Watch me."

The children watched. It was not faster.

"Good," said Coral. "That was very good and very fast."

"Thank you." Said Cadwallader. "Come here and see how I do it."

"Why?" asked Coral.

"Because it will be fun," replied Cadwallader.

"How will it be fun?" asked Emorix.

"We will play pickee pickee. That is the best gam,." replied Balboa.

"I have a good idea," said Coral. "Why don't we play blind pickee pickee?"

"How do you play that?" asked Cadwallader.

"You both turn your head around. Emorix and I will run forward until we are very close to you. Then we will say "ready". Then we get to play pickee pickee," replied Coral as she smiled.

Coral had thought of a plan. She whispered her plan so very softly in Emorix's ears that no one else could hear.

Emorix said: "Now, be careful both of you. The game is not peeky peeky. It is blind pickee pickee. Don't peek. That would be against the rules. Here is what we will do. I will count to three. You close your eyes as soon as I say three. Then we will run forward. We will stop. We will yell - Open your eyes!"

"That is when you open your eyes. Did you understand that?" asked Coral?

"Yes." said Balboa and Cadwallader. They seemed very excited.

"Good, let's do a practice run." Said Coral. "1…. 2…. 3…. Close your eyes."

Both Cadwallader and Balboa closed their eyes. They seemed very excited. They snickered and tittered. They teeheed and they heeheed. They shook with excitement. Their shaking made the ground shake.

Coral and Emorix checked carefully to make sure that the nasty tertiums were not looking. The children kept their eyes on them at all time. They noticed that sometimes the nasties cheated. They peeked through their petals. The children moved quickly forward.

"Can we look now?" yelled Balboa who was already peeking.

"No, not yet and stop peeking. If you do, you'll lose five points. You'll get to look later," yelled Coral.

"Is it later yet?" asked Cadwallader who did not want to lose any points.

"No, not yet," said Emorix. "You have to wait until we tell you."

"Okay, but be fast," replied Balboa.

The children advanced quite a bit forward. They were very careful not to come so close as to be within reach of the flowers. The children stopped.

They yelled, "Okay, you can look now."

"Ah!" Said Cadwallader who sounded disappointed. "You are too far for us to grab you."

"What did you say?" said Coral accusingly.

"He said you are not close enough to play pickee pickee with us," said Balboa quickly.

"That's right," said Cadwallader, trying to be sneaky. "I did not say – 'grab you' - I said 'play pickee pickee'."

"I thought you said, 'grab you'," said Coral.

"No!" said Cadwallader, bending his petals away from the children as if he was embarrassed.

"Okay," said Coral. She thought that the nasty tertiums might be dangerous. But they were not very nasty. At least they were not very good at being nasty. They did not seem to mean to be very nasty. Yet, they were very big. They were intent on picking the children. If that happened, it could be very dangerous.

"This was only a practice run," said Coral. "It would not have been right to do the best part of the game during a practice run."

Cadwallader nodded wisely. He understood that it was not right to do the game during the practice run. "You are right Coral. Can we do the real game of blind pickee pickee now?" he asked.

"Yes," said Coral, "are you ready?"

"Yes, we are ready," said the nasty tertiums as they tried to look both eager and sneaky at the same time.

"Okay, 1... 2... 3... Don't look. Don't peek. The game is about to start. Don't peek. You will lose five points if you do," yelled Emorix.

The children ran very fast. The nasties peeked. They tried to bend down. Coral had calculated the time it took them to bend down. She knew that they were quite slow even when they were trying to be the fastest they could be. She also knew that she and Emorix could run faster. They ran past the nasty tertiums. They kept running until they were out of reach on the other side of the nasty tertiums.

"Okay, you can look now," said Coral with the smile she has when she wins a game.

"No fair, you cheated. You went too far. Come back so we can pick you for our bouquet," yelled Balboa.

"That was not very nice of you to fool us that way. You come back. You lied to us. I will tell our mother if you don't," cried Cadwallader.

"Here we will close our eyes again and count to three. You can come back close to us. That would be a fun game," said Balboa with a sneaky smile.

"I don't think we will do that," said Emorix.

"You cheated. You must go back. It is in the rules. If you don't go back you will lose three points," said Cadwallader. "You will lose seven points," said Balboa. "You will lose all your point," threatened Cadwallader.

Coral liked points very much. She did not want to lose any points. For a second, she was tempted to go back. But she quickly recognized that it was a new trick. She stayed where she was. She argued that there was no rule that said the children would lose points if they did not go back.

"We had to run past you," Said Coral. "You were planning to pick us and hurt us. Your invitation to play pickee pickee was a trick. You only wanted to grab us."

"How did you know?" asked Balboa.

"We have secret and magical ways," said Emorix.

The Bouquet

"Okay - we like magic. We did not want to hurt you. We only wanted to pick you for our bouquet," said Cadwallader.

"What do you mean?" asked Coral.

"We are making a pretty bouquet for our mother. It is her birthday. We need more colors. You are so pretty and so colorful. You would make our bouquet look much better," said Balboa, hoping that the children would agree to become part of the bouquet.

"Yes," said Cadwallader. "We already have nine things for our bouquet. With the two of you we will have a dozen. This is how many we need."

Emorix knew that nine plus two makes eleven – not a dozen, which is twelve. He was tempted to correct Cadwallader's arithmetic, but he thought the better of it. If he corrected Cadwallader, the nasties would look for one more victim. This was not a good thing to do.

Coral immediately thought of the other nine. She asked who they were.

"Oh, they are very pretty." Said Balboa. "Some of them keep wiggling. That is pretty. We have a crocosmile, a kangadrool, four pretty pluckies: a mommy plucky, a baby plucky, a peeking plucky and a rubber plucky. We have a glowdog, a horse of a feather and a spunk."

The Nastytertiums have gathered many animals in a bouquet.
Will they be saved?
Who will save them?

The children felt sad for the poor prisoners of the nasties. They wondered whether the crocosmile was their partner and whether the kangadrool was their friend.

"Good," said Emorix who was thinking of a new plan. "Can we see them? I want to make sure that we would get along with them."

"Yes, all you have to do is come nearer," said Cadwallader. "You will get to see all of them."

"No," said Coral. "Stop trying to trap us. It will not work."

s

"And it is a good thing that it will not work," Said Emorix. "Because I have a much better idea. My idea will make your mother much happier than giving her a silly bouquet full of crocosmiles, kangadrools and other wigglely things. What if the crocosmile bit your mother's nose while she was smelling her bouquet? What if the pluckies were to pluck at her cheeks? Do you really think that your mother will like the smell of the spunk? Come, your mother will be very disappointed if you give her that bouquet for her birthday. She will be unhappy."

Emorix could be very persuasive and convincing. The nasty tertiums, who did not know that mothers like whatever their children give them for their birthday, suddenly looked very sad. They had planned very hard for their mother's birthday. They had used their best idea and their best work to trap all those animals. It had been difficult, but they had already gathered most of their bouquet. Emorix and Coral could see how sad and confused they looked. They did not like to see the nasty tertiums look so sad. Also, they wanted to free the prisoners of the flowers. Emorix continued with his plan.

"You had a very good plan." He said. "It was a very good idea. It is too bad that it could not work. What you need is another good idea. Think how happy your mother would be if she got special water from the Rainbow Falls. Flowers like water. We hear that the water of the Rainbow Falls is very sweet and very special. Your mother lives too far from the falls to get that special water. We could help you get water from the Rainbow Falls. It would make your mother very happy. Your mother would get the most special of all special presents."

"Yes," said Coral. While we go to get the special Rainbow Falls water you could write some very nice poems for your mother. She would like that too. Mothers like to get poems from their children on their birthday. Our mother does. It is her favorite present after her breakfast in bed."

"Yes" Said Emorix. "The water would be just like breakfast in bed."

"Goody! Goody!" said Cadwallader who was clapping his petals with excitement.

"Great! Greater than great!" said Balboa. "Water from the Rainbow Falls and poems from us would make mother very happy when we give the bouquet to her."

"No," said Coral. "Remember that the bouquet is not what you should give her. If you want the water, you have to forget about the bouquet. You have to let the animals go."

"Ha!" Said Balboa, who seemed to have trouble understanding that she should let go of the idea of the bouquet.

Cadwallader tried to help. "What if we told mother to smell them from far away. The animals could not bite her nose."

"No! No! No!" said the children, firmly. "This will not do. The best way to make your mother very happy is to give her water from the Rainbow Falls and to write a poem for her. Do you not agree?"

"Yes!" said the nasty tertiums. This would be the best present. She will like it. Maybe we can also have some of the water from Rainbow Falls for ourselves."

"Good," said Coral. "We can help you, but we will need you to help us also."

"Good, we like to help," said Cadwallader. "Whom do you want us to catch?"

"No one, we will need the kangadrool to carry the water. He has such a big pouch that your mother will get more water than any other nasty tertium mother ever got," said Emorix.

"Great, we will give back the kangadrool to help you."

"Good" said Coral. "We will also need the pluckies to swim on the water. They will send water towards the kangadrool's pouch. This will help us a lot. It will allow us to get more and better water for your mother."

"Great!" said the nasty tertiums. "Take the pluckies and the kangadrool and go."

"We will need more help." Said Coral. "We have never gone to the Rainbow Falls. We need someone to show us the way to make sure we get there as fast as possible. Let the crocosmile come with us. He can show us the best way."

"No," said Balboa. "You are trying to fool us. You will get all of our bouquet. Then you will run away and never come back. We will not have any present to give to our mother. The kangadrool and the four pluckies must know the way. They will show you how to get there."

"We agree," said Emorix. "We want to help you give your mother a very good present. But you must promise to let all of the bouquet free when we come back. This way everyone will be happy."

"That is fair," said Cadwallader. "If you help us get a good present for our mother, we will give you our bouquet."

"Good," said the children. We will help you get the best of all presents for your mother. May we speak with the crocosmile."

"Yes," said the nasty tertiums.

"How are you partner?" asked Coral.

"I am well." Replied the crocosmile. "But I am also sad. Time is extremely slow."

It was their partner and friend. The children were sad that he was a prisoner. At the same time, they were happy that they could help to free their friend.

Emorix said: " I will give your watch back to you. It may help the time pass faster."

"Thank you, but I would rather that you kept the watch. This way you will go and return faster. Don't forget to pull the red string for me."

"We are on our way... we will be back soon! Don't worry!" Yelled the children, as they rushed towards the Rainbow Falls with the kangadrool and with the pluckies in tow.

The impatience, a very pretty flower yelled: "Run. Hurry up. There is not much time." That is what impatiences like to say.

The children ran. The kangadrool hopped. The pluckies waddled. It is hard to run or to hop when you have web feet at the end of short legs. It is better to waddle.

As he ran, Emorix thought of pulling the string on the watch. He was thinking hard, trying to remember whether he should pull the red string or the gold one. He was not sure if in his excitement he could remember to do it right. He was also not quite sure whether it would be better for the time to go fast or for the time to go slow? There were lots of questions. There were lots of things to worry about. It is also hard to get things right when you are running. When you are happy to have saved the kangadrool and the pluckies. When you have to think about all the things you have to do to save the rest of your friends it is hard to concentrate specially when you have to make sure that nothing else that may be lurking in the florest could hurt you. Hurt your sister. Hurt your friends. It is so hard to concentrate when you think of too many things at the same time. He also was very tempted to look at all the marlavous and wondricus things that they were seeing as they ran through the florest. He did not. He had such an important thing to do.

"Thank you very much," said the kangadrool. "You saved me and you saved my friends. It is good what you are doing. I am very happy to be your friend."

"Thank you also." Said the mommy plucky. I am happy that you saved us also. You were very smart to fool the nasty tertiums.

They were so mean. We were very afraid to meet their mother. What if she was meaner than they were? She could have sniffed us to death. We are not very big. You can see that."

"We were very glad to help," said Coral. She was proud that she and her brother were heroes. She was glad they had saved the pluckies and the kangadrool. She was looking forward to saving the other animals in the bouquet.

The children and the animals ran as fast as they could. As they were getting close to the Rainbow Falls, the kangadrool said: "Stop! It would be dangerous for you to continue."

Coral was about to say that they had to continue to get the water. But she remembered that the kangadrool knew the ways of the florest better than the children did. Wisely she asked the kangadrool to explain.

"You have never seen the Rainbow Falls," said the kangadrool.

"The falls are so wondricus and marlavous that when you see the falls for the first time you should not be in a hurry. You will want to stay there and enjoy it all. That would be dangerous for our friends who are prisoners. We are in a hurry. We have to save all our other friends. Also, you will not have the time to enjoy the Rainbow Falls as much as you should when you see them for the first time. That would be unfair to you. It would also be unfair to the Rainbow Falls. They deserve to be seen for the first time when people are not in a hurry. They put on such a pretty show. I have an idea. You should stay here and wait for us. We have seen the Rainbow Falls many times before. It will be hard for us not to stay there for a long time. We will remember our friends who are in danger. No matter how much we want to stay and enjoy the Rainbow Falls, we will hurry. You wait here for us. Later, after we have freed our friends, we will come and enjoy the falls together. We may even have a picnic."

The children understood. They wanted to go. But they recognized that the kangadrool had said a very wise thing. They agreed. They sat down on a big fun flower seed in the shade of a mushyroom. They told the kangadrool and the pluckies to hurry. They wished them good luck.

The kangadrool was very glad that the children understood what he had said. He thought they were very wise children. He was about to tell them, but the impatience yelled: "Run. Hurry up. You are wasting time. Get going." The kangadrool remembered that he did not have much time. He told Emorix to pull on the red string on the watch so time would go fast. He hopped towards the Rainbow Falls as quickly as he could. The pluckies waddled as fast as they could behind him.

They reached the Rainbow Falls very quickly. What they saw there was extraordinarily extra. It was superdiffy magficognicient. It was even more than that. It was more than magic - it was imaginicallical. It was even better than that. I have never heard words that are good enough to tell you about the Rainbow Falls. We need brand new words for that.

The kangadrool was very tempted to stay and enjoy the Rainbow Falls. He was tempted not to return. The rubber plucky had to remind him of his promise. Using all the wisdom inside his four wisdom teeth, the kangadrool started to do his work.

He stood close to the water under the falls and made sure that the water would fall in his pouch. The pluckies were happy. They helped him by flapping their wings. They quacked a lot.

As soon as his pouch was full, the kangadrool quickly turned around in a way that he could not see the Rainbow Falls anymore. He started hopping away as fast as he could without spilling the water.

The children were waiting patiently under the mushyroom. They did not worry. They were sure that the kangadrool would come back with a pouch full of water. It was good for them to have a chance to rest. They had had a busy day so far. They felt that there would be more to come. They ate another choconut. They were relaxing quietly when they heard the hop hop and the waddle waddle in the distance. Soon they would see the kangadrool and the pluckies.

The hopping sounds grew louder. They heard a faint splash among the waddles. They knew that the kangadrool was carrying water. They looked as far down the path as they could. Soon they could see one waddling shape. Then there was another. Then there were two others. That was good but where was the kangadrool? Before they had time to worry, they saw him. At first it was only a small hopping figure. He was coming very fast for someone who had a belly full of water. They began to worry that the kangadrool may get a tummy ache from going so fast with a belly full of water.

The children stopped worrying when they remembered that the kangadrool was carrying the water inside the bag in his belly. It was not as if he had drunk too much water and was trying to run too fast. Also, they remembered that the kangadrool was used to that. It was his job to carry water for the beleaver. He had done that before. The kangadrool knew what he was doing. There would be no problems. At least there would be no problems unless the kangadrool started laughing and slapping his belly like he had done when he first met the children.

The children congratulated the kangadrool for his good work. They also congratulated the pluckies for helping their friend.

The impatience yelled: "Run. Hurry. Hurry."

They began walking towards the nasty tertiums as quick as they could without spilling the water. It did not take very long. As soon as they came in sight, they heard the nasty tertiums giggle from happiness. They welcomed the children and the kangadrool. Balboa spoke first.

"We are glad you came back so soon. We were afraid that you might just run away. We like your idea very much. I already wrote my poem for our mommy. Tell me if you like it. I think I will become a poet when I grow up.

Mommy, queen of the nasties
I think you are so pretty
Your stem is so stemmy
Your petals are so petally
Your seeds are so seedy
Your smell is so smelly
Mommy, queen of the nasties
I am glad you are my mommy."

The children did not want to tell Balboa that her poem was a bit silly. They did not want her to change her mind about releasing her prisoners.

Cadwallader who was also very exited interrupted before the children could speak any more. "I have one too! I have written one too! I think I will be a poet too!" He spoke. Then, hurriedly, he recited his poem.

"Mommy, princess of the nasties

I think you are so pretty
Your stem is so smelly
Your petals are so seedy
Your seeds are so stemmy
Your smell is so petally
Mommy, princess of the nasties
I am happy I was in your tummy."

Cadwallader then said: "It is not as good as Balboa's poem. She wrote hers first. She had the first choice, and she chose "queen". I had to use "princess". A princess is not as good as a queen. But the rest of it is very good. I am proud of it."

Coral recognized that Cadwallader's poem was even sillier than his sister's poem. Careful not to lie, she said: "You are right your mother will like both your poems very much. She will be very happy."

Coral spoke the truth. All mothers like their children's poems very much. The nasty tertiums were very happy and excited.

"Did you bring water from the Rainbow Falls?" asked Balboa.

"Yes, we did. Let our friends go." Said Emorix.

"No, you give the water to our mother first and then we will see. If she likes it, maybe we will let your friends go."

"That was not the deal we made." Said Coral. "You must let our friends go now. You promised. You will lose points if you don't. Worse, we will keep the water."

"If you keep the water, we will stomp our roots and throw a tantrum." Said Balboa. "We may hold our breath until we turn blue."

The children had trouble thinking of blue nasty tertiums. They did not want the nasty tertiums to throw a tantrum. They knew that tantrums were childish. They show that you were spoiled. Threatening tantrums is a very bad way to try to get what you want. The nasty tertiums were being very bad. They were breaking their promise to let the prisoners go. They were being nasty.

The kangadrool who was wise and did not like tantrums, had a good idea. "Here" he said to the nasty tertiums. "You have been working very hard. You must be tired. Let me give you a little bit of the Rainbow Falls water. It will refresh you."

He was brave. He went close to the nasty tertiums. He went near their roots. They could have caught him again. He started pouring some of the water from the Rainbow Falls. The water went into the ground and reached the roots of the nasty tertiums. Gradually, the water went through the roots and up the stem of both flowers.

It happened so fast that the children, who had seen many strange and wondricus things that day, had trouble believing it. Both Balboa and Cadwallader grew taller. They grew taller by the height of one and a half kangadrool. Their leaves became greener. The leaves became greener than green. The petals looked as if they were alive. Their orange color became even brighter than the orange color of oranges that comes out of the stockings on Christmas morning. Both flowers grew to be more beautiful than anything the children had ever seen in their life.

"That is very good water. It is so sweet and nourishing. Thank you very much." Said Balboa.

"I feel very good. Quick, we must free those poor animals. We are so sorry. I hope we did not hurt them." Cadwallader slowly lowered the rest of the prisoners to the ground. He apologized to them. He also thanked the kangadrool, the pluckies and the children. The prisoners were very happy to be free. They forgave the nasty tertiums. The crocosmile thanked his partners. He was very proud that his special partners were heroes. He hoped they would get a big shiny medal. Everybody was happy.

The children had seen the magic of the water from the Rainbow Falls. You remember when I told you that the crocosmile used to be a crocogrump. He had become a crocosmile when he had tasted the honey made by the monkbees. The same thing had happened. The children had just seen the water change the nasty tertiums into nicey tertiums.

The crocosmile introduced the children to the glowdog, the spunk and to the horse of a feather.

The horse of a feather was very strange. He had a big and pretty green feather on top of his head. Different pieces of him kept falling off - the head, then the tail, one leg and then another leg. He would put a fallen part back on. Immediately, another part would fall off. The children felt sorry for him. They offered to help. He said: "Don't bother. I am a horse of a feather. You have heard that birds of a feather flock together. We, horses of a feather don't stick together. Then he laughed. That is how we are. It is awkward. Sometimes it makes me sad. We cannot go to rodeos. We cannot go to races. It would be too dangerous. We could hit somebody else."

Emorix had a good idea. He suggested that the horse of a feather go to the Rainbow Falls and bathe in the water. If the water had so much magic, maybe, it could help the horse stick together. The horse of a feather thought it was a good idea. He thanked the children again. He said: "Excuse me." He ran towards Rainbow Falls as fast as all his falling parts allowed.

Coral reminded everybody that it was Balboa and Cadwallader's mother's birthday. They found her just behind her children. Balboa and Cadwallader sang 'Happy Birthday' to her. The kangadrool poured the water over her roots. Everybody very much enjoyed watching the mother of the nasty tertiums become transformed into a mother nicey tertium. The change made her very happy. She said she felt rested. It is tiring to be a nasty all the time. It is much more enjoyable to be nice.

Then, the nicey tertium children recited their poems. They even remembered to replace the words "queen and princess of the nasties" with "queen and princess of the nicies". The mother was even happier with the poems than she was with everything else. She hugged her children. She gave them each a very big kiss and told them how happy they had made her.

Balboa and Cadwallader told their mother that they had made new friends. They introduced Coral, Emorix and all the former prisoners to her. The mother nicey tertium was very happy that her children had made so many new friends. Even the impatience thought that this was time well spent. She had never ever had a thought like that before!

Standor's House

Coral and Emorix wanted to go to Rainbow Falls very much. But it would soon start to get dark. The crocrosmile told them that they should wait until morning. They would have more time to enjoy the Rainbow Falls. The children remembered that Standor's wife would be waiting for them at her house. They did not want to be late. They did not want him to worry. They also knew that it was not polite to be late. Their mother had taught them to be polite. She had taught them to be on time. The children agreed with the crocrosmile. They said goodbye to everybody.

They turned around. They started on the way back to Standor's house. The glowdog, who was grateful to be free, said: "Wait for me. It will get dark soon. I will go with you. When it gets dark, I glow. I may be able to help you find your way." Everybody agreed. They thought it was a good idea. Coral, Emorix and the glowdog started walking back towards the big rock.

While they were walking back to Standor's house the glowdog told the children his story. He had wanted to become a growl dog but he had gotten the letters all mixed up. Also, he had lent the "R" to a toy company. Instead of a growl dog he had become a glowdog. At first, he was disappointed. Later, he thought about it. He thought it was much better. He explained that the glow came from the smile in his eyes when he wagged his tail. Wagging his tail made him very happy. It made him feel all warm inside. The happiness and the warmth made his eyes shine with a bright light.

The impatience said: "Hurry up. There is not much time. It will get dark soon."

Emorix pulled the red cord on the crocrosmile watch. Time went very quickly. They passed by the big rock that won't do a thing.

Coral checked the map that she had made. They looked around and saw the potrose garden. They walked to it. They remembered to take a deep breath to smell the perfume from the flowers. Just like Standor had told them to do. They were happy they did that. The smell was sweet. It reminded them of the best perfume their grandmother wore. They walked back four hundred and twenty paces. That did put them close to the biggest dizzy. At the biggest dizzy, they turned around once. After that, they walked straight ahead until they came to a small pond. As they neared the shore of the small pond, they could smell the sweet smell of their grandmother's best perfume again. There were potroses in the air.

It was getting dark. The glowdog wagged his tail. He looked straight ahead. A very bright and warm light came from the smile in his eyes. He would have looked like a four-legged, tail-wagging flashlight except that he had two eyes. He looked like a four-legged, tail-wagging double flashlight.

The children could see very far. They could see a very scary thing. They saw the back of a huge porky-u-pine. It was just ahead of them. They wondered if it was as dangerous as it appeared. They noticed that the back of the porky-u-pine was covered with rose petals. Coral checked her map again to make sure they were not lost. That is when she noticed the note she had written. It reminded her to be careful not to touch the big potrose thorns that were on the outside of the hut. They were not seeing the back of a porky-u-pine. The children and the glowdog had arrived at Standor's house.

They found the door. It was made from the biggest rose petal they had ever seen. They knocked on the door. Mrs. Standor opened the door. She was with her husband. He said: "Come in, I am glad that you have found my house. You must be tired. Come and sit down. We will talk about the adventures you had today."

Standor saw the glowdog. He asked him to come in also. The glowdog was happy to be invited inside the house. He wagged his tail. Light came out from his eyes.

The inside of Standor's house was not very big but it was very pretty. To Coral it looked like a dollhouse. Emorix thought it looked like a fort. There was a nice purple table made from half the petal of a prosy. There were four chairs. The chairs were red. They were carved from cherries. There were three lamps. These were glowpuppies. Mrs. Standor would say "nice puppies" and the lamps would wag their tail and make light. In the living room there was a couch and two rocking chairs. The couch was yellow and shiny. It was made from the largest banana the children had ever seen. The rocking chairs were white. They were made from the cups of two lollies of the volley. The two beds were white. They were made from the petals of a dizzies. The pillows were made from the fluff of some "dandy-lie-ons". They were soft and cuddly. You could lie on them.

On the walls there were one hundred and many more pictures of Ronkian children who had a great big smile. They were the children that Standor had cured. The house looked very pretty and very comfortable. There was also a picture of Standor's police school certificate and three frames of Mrs. Standor's university degrees.

Standor asked the children to sit at the table. Mrs. Standor served them a glass of choconut milk and some fun flower seeds dipped in the honey from the monkbees. As soon as they tasted the honey, the children knew why the crocrosmile was always smiling. Standor said that he had thought of going to the bakery of the beleaver, but he did not think that the children would like to eat mud pies. The children agreed.

Standor said: "I hear that you had a very busy day. You made many new friends. You became a special partner of the crocrosmile. You saved all the prisoners that Balboa and Cadwallader had captured. I hear that you even used some of the water from Rainbow Falls to change the nasty tertiums into nicey tertiums. You have stopped them from making trouble for everyone walking along that path. My wife and I are very happy. We are very proud of what you did. You are good children. We are glad that you have come to visit our florest."

The children were surprised that Standor knew everything that they had done that day. They told Standor they were surprised that he knew so much about their adventure.

Standor explained: "When you left me that morning, I asked one of my friends, Little Bird, to follow you. I had to go and cure a sick child. I could not go with you. I did not want you to get lost or to get into trouble. It would not be nice of me to welcome you in our florest and not protect you. All day, Little Bird flew over your head. He is so small, and he flew so high that you did not see him. I told him to keep a close look on you. I told him to come and get me or my wife if you got into trouble. Little bird brought his cousin, Hoot Bird, with him. Hoot Bird is a special bird. He can only be seen at night. During the day, Little Bird and Hoot Bird followed you. Every hour, Little Bird flew back to me. He told me what you were doing while Hoot Bird stayed near you to make sure you were not in danger. I know everything you did. You could say: "A little bird told me."

The children wondered if that was the same little bird their grandmother knew. She often said that a little bird told her things.

Standor opened the window and told the children to look outside in the branches of the nearest potrose. They could see two big yellow eyes and two tiny dots beside the big yellow eyes. "This is

Hoot Bird, and this is Little Bird." Said Standor. "They protected you all day."

"Thank you very much." Said the children.

"You are welcome. We were glad to help." Hooted, Hoot Bird. He had been taught to be polite by his mother. "We enjoyed watching your adventure. You are very nice. You are very brave. You are very smart. I thank you for making the nasty tertiums into nicey tertiums. I thank you for saving our friends. That was very nice of you."

"You are welcome." Said Emorix who was also polite. His mother had taught him that.

"Goodbye and good night." Peeped Little Bird with his little bird voice. Both cousins flew away.

The children had many questions to ask Standor. They wanted to know everything they could about the wondricus and marlavous things in the Florest of Ronkledongding. They asked Standor. He was proud that the children were interested in his florest. People like to tell visitors about the place where they live. Standor agreed to answer their question.

Coral spoke first. "Please tell us Mr. Standor, how do you make the flowers so big?"

"We make sure we do not make them small like you do where you live." Said Standor.

That made sense to the children.

"Tell us Mr. Standor, what do you do?" Said Emorix.

"I am a chief of the Ronkian people. We are very few Ronkians. As you can see, we are very small. We live here in the Florest of Ronkledongding. The florest is at the bottom of the world. It is the place where rainbows are born. It is where they start. Very few people come here and very few people know us. We like visitors. But we like them to be good visitors. For that reason, we have asked our friends the leprechauns to put a pot of gold at the end of rainbows. They did. When greedy people chase rainbows, they always go to the end of the rainbow to look for the gold. They never come to the beginning of the rainbow. They leave us alone. Only nice people are wise enough to realize that whatever would start a rainbow would be better than gold. You have to be especially nice to think of going to the beginning of the rainbow and away from the pot of gold. You have to know what is the most important. This way we get fewer visitors. They are nicer visitors also. We have to be careful. We would not want someone to come and cut all our flowers. We would not want someone to build big hotels and restaurants at the Rainbow Falls. We want to keep its natural beauty.

I am also a doctor. I specialize in curing children and in fixing broken feet and knees. If you are ever sick, come and see me. I will make you smile. That will send the sickness away.

The children thought about Standor's way of curing children. They knew that when they were sick, they always smiled more at the end of their sicknesses than during their sickness. They had always thought that they were smiling because they had stopped being sick. What Standor had said made the children wonder if it was not the reverse. Maybe the sickness had stopped because they smiled. That also made sense to them.

"Wow!" Said Emorix. "You are the chief of the Ronkian people. It must be nice to be the chief of a whole people."

Standor corrected him. "I did not say I was the chief of the Ronkians. I said I was a chief. There is a difference. Let me explain. All Ronkians are chiefs. Long before 'ago' we recognized that each one of us had something special to give to the others. Each one of us could and had to help with different problems. Some were better for one kind of situation. Others were better for another kind of situation. That is when we decided that life would be better if we all were chiefs. We do not take turns. We just let the type of situation decide who is the best to lead us at that moment. The others help that leader because we know that things will be better for all of us when we work together. For the Ronkians everyone is a chief because everyone helps as best as he can." For example, Mrs. Standor is a scientist. If we need to understand something difficult or if we need to discover something new, she is our chief for that.

"Tell us about the Florest of Ronkledongding." Said Coral. Standor smiled with his eyes and he smiled with his mouth. He looked up towards the moon and said in a singing voice:

There are marlavous and wondricus things
That live in the Florest of Ronkledongding.
There's a one-legged bird with only five wings
And there's a great big rock that won't do a thing

There are marlavous and wondricus things
that live in the Florest of Ronkledongding.
There is fluit juice that sprouts from the spring
and there's a beleaver who thinks he's a king.

There are marlavous and wondricus things
that live in the Florest of Ronkledongding.
There are nasties that grab everything
and there are potroses that smell like gold rings.

There are marlavous and wondricus things
that live in the Florest of Ronkledongding.
There are monkbees that cure with their sting
and the flowers make the weather smell like spring.

There are marlavous and wondricus things
that live in the Florest of Ronkledongding.
There is a kangadrool who hops to a spring,
and there is a crocrosmile that pulls on a string.

There are marlavous and wondricus things
that live in the Florest of Ronkledongding.
The lollies of the volley have bells on a string
and rainbows start whenever they ring.

"That's what we say about our florest. I guess that we will have to change what we say about the nasties now that you have made them nice." Chuckled Standor.

"That was a very good thing you did. You see, Emorix, at that time you and Coral were chiefs. The kangadrool was a chief when he went to get the water. Everyone can be a chief. Everyone is a chief when he is doing good things." Emorix understood.

He asked Standor why he said "marlavous and wondricus" instead of "marvelous and wonderful"?

Standor explained that sometimes things are so strange and magical that an ordinary word is not good enough. New words are needed. He explained that television was a new word that did not exist when their grandmother was a child. Rocket ship was also a new word that had to be made up to describe something new and exiting. All the words we use today were new someday. Some were made up a long time ago. Some were made even before sandwiches were invented. They had to make a new word for that too. We Ronkians have read all the dictionaries to find the correct words to describe the things in the florest. We did not always find the words that sounded like we felt about the things in our florest. Perhaps it is because the people who wrote the dictionaries had never been in the florest and had never seen such things. The things that live in the florest are so unique that we need unique words to describe them. This is why we had to make up our own new words.

The children did not find that hard to understand.

Coral had another question to ask. "Tell me." She spoke. "How big is the Florest of Ronkledongding?"

"It is just big enough to hold all the wonderful things we need and small enough for us to enjoy them. The florest is just right. It is 78 camel-otters long and just a few more camel-otters wide."

"What is a camel-otter?" She asked.

Standor smiled as he explained that a camel-otter was the way the Ronkians measured distance. "It is the exact distance a camel will travel away from an otter until he stops seeing the otter. The otter is small. It is a bit short in distance. The camel must travel backward to keep his eyes on the otter. Everybody knows that camels are not very fast when they go backwards. They are actually quite slow. It takes a long time for a camel to travel a camel-otter, but he does not travel very far. A camel-otter can be measured in time - it is a long time. When it is measured in distance - it is a short distance. In the florest we measure it both ways. If we want to get somewhere fast, we use the distance way. If we want to get there slowly, we use the time way."

Emorix, who was very good at distances in school said: "I never heard of a camel-otter either. It seems to be a strange way to measure things."

"Yes." Said Standor. "It is different. But we are not the only ones to use strange ways to measure things. I have heard that there are places where people use the length of a king's foot or the length of his thumb to measure distance. I have also heard that some people use the behavior of a knot on a rope in water to say how fast they are going. I am even told that there is another place that uses the weight of a container of water to tell how heavy things are. These ways are a bit strange to us."

"I get your point." Said Emorix. "The important thing is that people understand each other."

"I really like the fact that you use the same measure to tell how long it takes to go somewhere and how far it is. I would think that a camel-otter is not very far. When you want to speak of very very long distances, like the distance to our house. Do you use camel-otters or do you have another measure?"

Standor replied: "Yes, for things that are very far away, we use the otter-camel. It is much longer. It is the distance a camel has to travel away from an otter until the otter no longer sees the camel. Because the camel is so much bigger than the otter, the camel has to travel very far before the otter stops seeing it. That distance is very far away. An otter-camel is much longer than a camel-otter. But this time it is the otter that has to keep watching the camel. The camel can travel forward. We all know that a camel can travel forward much faster than he can travel backward. An otter-camel takes less time than a camel-otter. This is good. If we want to go somewhere that is far away but we want to go there fast, we use the time of an otter-camel. If we want to go very far, we use the distance of an otter-camel.

"I like the way you do that." Said Emorix who was a little sad that Coral had reminded him how far they were from their home and from their parents.

Standor sensed that the children were thinking of their family. He also knew that they had had a wonderful adventure in the florest.

"I enjoy your company and you have made many friends. Will you visit with us for a long while?" Said Standor. "What I said is wrong. Good visitors never stay long enough. If you visited with us, no matter how long you stayed, it would not be a long time. It would never be long enough. You are so nice. We like you so much. Any length of stay would be too short. I should have asked if you will stay with us for many days?"

"That would be nice." Said Coral. "But we will have to go back to our home. Our parents must be worried about us. They must be very sad."

"I understand." Said Standor. "But it will be difficult. I know there is a 'way out'. I know where it is and how it works. You found the 'way in'. It is the only way to come here - on the back of the rainbow. We are very proud that rainbows start here. Rainbows are our gift to the world. It is our way to make people, who cannot be here, feel the marlavous and wondricus ways of the Florest of Ronkledongding. I cannot tell you the 'way out'. The 'way out' works only if you find it by yourself."

Maybe it is possible to climb back on the rainbow? Asked Coral hopefully.

"No, the blue band is too slippery, and the other bands are not solid enough." Said Standor. "That is not the way. We have had a few visitors in the past. Most have left after they found out how to do it. Some have come back to visit us. We are so happy here that we hardly ever think of the 'way out' ourselves. Some of us have never bothered to find out where it is and how it works. Others don't bother to remember. They think that remembering something they will not use may clutter their mind. It may make them forget the smell of the flowers or the name of a friend. We know they are wrong. We know that there is enough room in their head to remember everything they would want to remember. But they are happy thinking that they are being smart that way."

"We will try to find the 'way out' tomorrow." Said Emorix while he was yawning.

Standor noticed that the children were tired. They had had a very busy day. They were planning to go back home. They would need lots of rest for the long trip. He suggested they go to bed. He told them they could sleep in the bedroom. He, Standor would sleep on the couch with his wife in a sleeping bag made from the pods of a "sweet peace". The glowdog said good night and left the house.

They all went to bed. The children went to sleep right away. They dreamt of their dog. They dreamt of their parents. They dreamt of their new friends and they dreamt of all the marlavous and wondricus things they had seen today. Those were wondricus and happy dream. Standor dreamt of curing children. His wife dreamt of having children as nice as Emorix and Coral. These were their favorite dreams. They liked children.

The Start of the Second Day

The children slept well. They woke up. As soon as they woke up, the sun woke up. It would be a beautiful sunny day. Standor was already up. He had prepared breakfast for them and Mrs. Standor. The children had seven and a little bit more glasses of fluit juice. It tasted marlavous. They ate the flesh from a choconut and some more honey from the monkbees.

There was a knock at the door. It was their friend the kangadrool. He had brought some mud doughnuts with dry holes for their breakfast. It was a lucky thing that the children had already eaten their breakfast. They thanked the kangadrool, but they did not have to eat the mud doughnuts. They thought that was a good thing.

The kangadrool said he had wondricus news. He had a new job. He would take water from the Rainbow Falls to the nicey tertiums. They enjoyed being nice so much more than being nasty that they wanted Rainbow Falls water everyday.

He said it was a better job than his other job for the beleaver. This job let him go to the Rainbow Falls everyday. That made him very happy.

The spunk also came to visit. She wanted to say thank you again. She and the crocrosmile had worked all night by the light of the glowdog to make pretty medals from the petals of a "Merry Gold" for the children. The medals said, "To our Heroes - Coral and Emorix." The children were very pleased. It was the first time they had a shiny hero medal. The spunk asked them to come outside.

The children were surprised when they opened the door. Many of their new friends were waiting. They had come to wish them a happy morning and to watch their heroes get their medal. The crocrosmile was there. All the pluckies were there. The glowdog was wagging his tail. Even the one-legged bird with only five wings was there. He was standing on the head of the mummy pluckie. It made her look as if she was wearing a funny hat. Even the lover was there. He had a very big smile. The smile was bigger than the size of his big boots. He was with a very pretty lady. The children guessed that she was the loved one. The children were happy that he had found her. Little Bird was also there. The children guessed that Hoot Bird would also be there but was invisible. They remembered that Standor said that Hoot Bird could not be seen during the day. The children were very glad to see so many of their new friends.

The crocrosmile stood up on his tail. He looked at all the animals. He began a long speech about how his special partners had done so many wondricus things. He told everyone how his partners had saved him and the other prisoners. Then he asked the children to come forward. He gave them each a medal and a very big kiss on both cheeks. The children had never been kissed by a crocrosmile. It felt funny. But they were glad to get the medal. They thanked everybody.

All the animals cheered. The children were very proud. They also felt very good about all the love that their new friends were showing.

In the distance they heard a faint shout. "Wait for me! Wait for me! I want to thank them too." Then there was the sound of a galloping horse.

When the horse arrived near Standor's house, no one knew who he was. No one remembered meeting him before. Who was that stranger? Why was he coming to thank the children? They did not know him.

He was a very pretty horse. He was big. He had a golden color skin like their cousin Alison's palomino. This was a pretty horse. He was even prettier than the palomino. He had two big feathers on top of his head. One was blue and very pretty. The other was green and very fancy. He reminded the children of the horses at the circus.

"Thank you, my friends. Thank you very much." Said the horse. Then he looked puzzled and sad. "Don't you recognize me? You saved me yesterday."

The horse looked just a little bit familiar to the children. They did not think he was the one they had saved the day before. That horse had only one feather on top of his head. He also kept falling apart. This horse had two feathers. He had run all the way to Standor's house without losing his head - or any other part of his body. This could not be the same horse.

The horse explained: "Just yesterday I was the horse of a feather. I was the horse that did not stick together. I did what Emorix told me to do. I went to the Rainbow Falls. It was very pretty. I stayed very long to look at everything. That is why I am late. At the Rainbow Falls I drank the water. I even bathed in the water. A very strange and wondricus thing happened. I grew another feather." He said proudly. "I am no longer a horse of a feather. I am no longer the sort of horse that does not stick together. I am a horse of two feathers. Everybody knows that horses of two feathers stick together. I no longer lose parts of me all the time. It is better to stick together. I am so happy. I thank you very much."

All the animals and Standor agreed that horses of two feathers always stuck together. They knew that. They had never seen a horse of two feathers fall apart. So, it must be true. It was also true that they had never seen a horse of two feathers. Just the same, they knew deep inside them that horses of two feathers would always stick together. They were happy for the horse. The children were also happy for the horse. They knew that it was better to stick together.

"I think you have a problem." Said the spunk. "One of your feathers is green and the other feather is blue. My sister told me that: "Blue and green should never be seen together, except in the washing machine."

I am afraid that you will have to spend all your life inside a washing machine."

Everybody had heard that. Coral's mother had told the same thing to the children's father. She told him that every time he dressed to go and play golf.

Everyone agreed that the horse was not ugly. He was very pretty. They worried that the horse would be unhappy inside a washing machine.

When she saw that the horse was sad, the spunk wanted to cheer him up. She said: "Maybe you can come out at night when no one can see you."

That did not make the horse happy. The horse did not think he was pretty anymore.

It was Coral who had the right idea. She said: "Look at the pretty flowers behind you. What do you call them."

"We call them bluelets." Said Standor with a smile. He had guessed what Coral was going to say.

"Are they pretty?" Asked Coral.

Everyone agreed that the bluelets were very pretty.

"Look." Said Coral. "They have blue petals and green leaves, and they are not in the washing machine. If bluelets with green leaves can be seen, a pretty golden horse with green and blue feathers can also be seen outside the washing machine."

Everyone agreed that this had to be true. The horse started to smile again. He was happy again. The spunk apologized for worrying the horse.

All was well again.

Emorix could hardly wait to tell his father that his golf clothes were just as pretty as a bluelet!

Much time had passed very quickly. The kangadrool and all the others remembered they had to go. The kangadrool had to go to work. Others had to go to school. Others had to go to visit their uncles and their aunts. They said goodbye to the children and went down the different paths away from Standor's house. The children yelled: "Thank you very much. It was nice of all of you to come and visit. Have a good day. See you later. Thank you for the medals".

The Balamoose

The horse stayed with the children. He was very happy. He was grinning from feather to feather. He wanted to do something for the children. He offered them a ride.

"That is a good idea." Said Emorix, who had never ridden a horse of two feathers. Both children had ridden horses before. Their cousin Alison had shown them how to ride. Going by horse would be faster. It would also be fun.

"Don't worry." Said the horse. "I do not fall to pieces anymore. I am as solid as a horse of two feathers. You will be safe with me."

Coral said: "I am not worried about you falling apart. I am worried that if we ride you, we would be going too fast. We may miss some of the pretty things in the florest."

"Yes, there is that possibility." Said Emorix. "But think. We did not get to see the Rainbow Falls yesterday. Everyone says it is one of the best places in the florest. I would like to go there today. It would be fun. The horse could get us there very quickly." We could spend more time there. Emorix was also hoping to get to ride fast like a cowboy on a horse.

The impatience shouted: "Go fast. Do not dally. There is no time to lose. Let's get on with it. What are you waiting for?

Standor told the children that the impatience flower always said that. It was too impatient. It was always in a rush. He told the children to ignore it.

Coral understood. She also wanted to ride fast. But she did not want to miss out on all the wondricus things that would be on their way. However, she agreed with Emorix that the Rainbow Falls should be the first place to visit that day. It would be exiting.

Standor agreed that the Rainbow Falls would be the best place to visit. He was glad that Coral understood that when you go too fast sometimes you miss some of the best things. He was also glad to hear that the children wanted to ride a fast horse. That can also be a nice experience. Life is not only about smelling flowers. It is also about doing things. It is about getting places. This is how the children got so many wonderful adventures. He thought that going by horse could be fun.

Standor lent the children his saddle. It was made from strumberry flowers. It was a strong flower. It was also pretty. It looked like a saddle for fast riding. It was white.

Standor said that today there were no sick children in the florest. He explained that there would not be room for him on the horse. He would go with them. He would ride his own animal. Standor called for his ride. The children could see what they thought was a small zebra run very fast to the house. They were not sure it was a zebra. It looked a bit like a zebra, but it was moving so fast. It was difficult to tell. It looked like it had stripes. Some seemed to be going up and down like the stripes on a zebra. Other stripes looked like they were going from front to back. The children thought the zebra looked like a black and white checkerboard. Emorix thought it looked like the winner's flag at car races. He knew that this animal would be very fast.

"What kind of animal is this?" He asked.

Standor said it is a zoom-by. They have long stripes for going forward and backward. They also have up and down stripes to help them jump. The children were impressed. This was another marlavous creature from the florest. The zoom-by said hello to the horse. He told the horse that his feathers looked pretty.

The horse said: "It is good that they are blue and green. They look like bluelets. Bluelets don't have to live inside a washing machine."

The zoom-by agreed. The zoom-by introduced himself to the children. His mother had taught him to be polite.

Standor put another stromberry saddle on the zoom-by. The children got on the horse and Standor got on the zoom-by. Emorix was exited. He thought that the zoom-by had a name to go fast. Maybe it could zoom! Maybe it would zoom by.

They started riding down the path towards the Rainbow Falls. At first they went slowly. Then they went a little faster. The horse and the zoom-by were trotting up and down. Then they started going much faster. They were doing a full gallop. It was exiting.

They passed an impatience. It yelled at them. "There you go. Faster! Go! Go! Go!"

This time the children agreed. They were riding very fast.

They passed the great big rock very quickly. They turned to the left. Standor showed them a new path to the Rainbow Falls. It was wide and pretty. There were many pretty flowers along the path. All the flowers were of only one kind. They were lollies of the volley.

"We call it the lolly of the volley pathway." Yelled Standor as he rushed forward. They were riding so fast that the monkbees did not even try to hit them with a choconut. The group raced towards the sharp curve in the path.

It was exiting. The children and Standor were going very fast. They were running almost as if they were in a race. They took the curve at great speed.

There was great danger ahead. There was the biggest lolly of the volley right in the middle of the road. That was not the danger. The children and Standor were very good riders. They could go around the stem of the lolly of the volley. The danger was that there was a great big thing that was whirling around and around the stem. The children and Standor were riding from the North. The big thing was whirling from the South.

Whirl! Whirl! Faster Whirl! Louder Whirl!

Clop a di clop! Clop a di clop! Faster Clop a di clop! Louder Clop a di Clop!

Whirl! Clop a di clop! Whirl! Clop a di clop! Faster Whirl! Faster Clop a di clop! Louder Whirl! Louder Clop a di Clop!

They were going to crash. It is bad to crash with a big whirling thing. It is worse to crash when the only doctor in the florest is going to crash with you.

It is a good thing that the zoom-by has special brakes. It is also good that horses of two feathers also have special brakes. They put on their brakes. Parachutes opened behind them. They stopped. They stopped just in time. There was only the space of the thickness of an eardrum between them and the whirling thing.

The Balamoose cannot go anywhere.

His suspenders are stuck in a lolly of the volley!

Standor and some of his elf friends brush his teeth and wash him every day!

How will that get resolved?

To be safer, they backed up nine paces plus another half a pace..

"Wow! That was exiting!" Said Emorix.

"Yes, it was exiting. What is that?" Said Coral.

Standor explained. "This is Whizzy, the balamoose. I had forgotten he was here. He does not whirl all the time. Sometimes he hops as if he was on a Jolly Jumper. It is sad. He has a big problem. He wears suspenders. They are hanging from the big lolly of the volly. Sometimes he goes around the stem too often. The elastics from the suspenders get very tight. When they get too tight, they unwind and whirl him around. Just like you see. There is nothing we can do. We will have to wait. He will stop whirling."

The children felt sad for the poor balamoose. It is a good thing that Emorix thought of pulling the red cord from the crocosmile's watch. Time went very fast. The twirling stopped soon. The balamoose looked very dizzy. He looked very sad.

He said: "There it is. The florest is twirling around me again.

This florest should be called 'the Florest of Ringawirling'.

That's what I think. It twirls around too much. I am so dizzy. I am so sad."

The children looked at the scene. If it were not so sad, it would be funny. Whizzy was very bow-legged. He wore thick green socks up to his knees. The suspenders were tied to the stem of the lolly of the volley. All Whizzy could do was walk around in circles under the lolly of the volley. The balamoose looked very unhappy. The children wanted to help Whizzy. Standor could see what they were thinking. He explained to them that he did not think they could fix the problem.

Everybody had tried everything. Nothing had worked. Not even drinking the water from the Rainbow Falls. They had given Whizzy some water to drink. They had washed him with the water. They had brushed his teeth with the water. They even poured water all over him. That day he caught a cold. They had washed his feet with the water. His toenails grew longer – nothing else. Nothing had worked. Whizzy was still tied to the lolly of the volley. He was a prisoner. The magic of the Rainbow Falls water did not work on the balamoose.

The balamoose was very discouraged. Everybody was very discouraged. Everyday they brought him food and something to drink. Many came to visit him. But the balamoose was the saddest creature in the whole Florest of Ronkledongding.

Coral said: "Mister balamoose, why do you wear suspenders?"

He said: "I wear them to keep my antlers on my head. When I don't wear suspenders, the antlers fall off."

Coral remembered learning in school that a moose, a deer, and a caribou lose their old antlers every year. They grow new one soon after losing the old ones. Many animals with antlers do that. Maybe the same thing happened to the balamoose. Maybe the antlers were supposed to come off. Maybe the balamoose was trying to fight nature. She told the balamoose what she knew. The balamoose was interested. He did not know that some animals with antlers shed them once a year.

"This cannot be true." He said. "Antlers are what makes a balamoose a balamoose. I do not want to lose my antlers. I do not want to stop being a balamoose. My mother told me balamooses should be balamooses. A balamoose is what a balamoose should be."

Coral said: "It even happens to children, two years ago some of my teeth fell off. That made way for grown-up teeth to grow instead."

"Think about it." Said Emorix. "Today you are a prisoner. You cannot walk in the florest. You cannot go and visit your uncles and your aunts. You cannot go into the lakes to swim. You cannot go and eat the tall grass. You are sad. Many times, you twirl around, and you become dizzy. Is that being a balamoose? You have your antlers. You look like a balamoose. But, because of the suspenders you cannot do anything that a balamoose likes to do. Do you like spinning around the lolly of the volley more than running with your friends? Is it more important to look like a balamoose? Or is it more important to act like a balamoose?"

The balamoose still looked sad. He also looked as if he was thinking as hard as he had ever thought in all of his life.

He was proud of his antlers. But... he really would like to be able to do all the fun things he used to do before his antlers fell off. Maybe Coral was right. Losing antlers could be a thing that a balamoose is supposed to do. But the antlers are so pretty. They are so balamoosey. He did not want to lose them. But... he was tired of being sad and being dizzy all the time.

Standor spoke. "My friend, these are very smart and very wise children. I believe what Coral said. Your antlers fell off. You worked very hard to put them back on your head. I think what she said might be true."

"I think that Emorix asked some very important questions. It is more important to act like what you are than to look like what you are. You are a balamoose. You are a balamoose when you have antlers. You are also a balamoose when you don't have antlers. You think you look pretty with your antlers on your head. They are all tied up with suspenders. Antlers with suspenders do not look very balamoosey to me. They look like antlers and suspenders on top of a balamoose head. I think you would be a better balamoose if you could do what a balamoose is supposed to do. I also think that you would be happier."

The children were surprised. They knew that Standor was a very kind man. They were surprised that he had spoken so directly to the balamoose.

The balamoose bowed his head. The balamoose was good at bowing things. The head was one of those things the balamoose was good at bowing. He scratched his legs to the ground. He looked like he was moping. He looked like he was sulking. Maybe he was thinking. Maybe it was a moping and sulking kind of thinking. He looked embarrassed. He looked sad. He also looked like a sad balamoose with suspenders and antlers on top of his head.

He looked at Standor who was on his left from the corner of his right eye. He looked at the children who were on his right from the corner of his left eye. The balamoose could look cross-eyed. He said that it was true that he had been sad not being able to go and do all the things he used to do. He told the children how much fun it was to be in the middle of a swamp and to eat grass. Eating the grass of the Florest of Ronkledongding was very good. It was sweet grass. When the grass was wet with swamp water, it was very tender and very tasty. He told Standor that he did miss walking in the florest. He did miss running and playing. He missed visiting other animals.

He said that it was true he was proud of his antlers. Maybe Coral was right. Maybe a balamoose's antlers do fall off. Then he smiled. He just had an idea. "If it is true what Coral that a balamoose's antlers fall off. It must also be true as she said that antlers grow again."

"Yes." Said Coral. "I think your antlers will grow again. They should even grow bigger. Every year the new antlers should have one more point than the year before. In a few years, you will have so many more points than now that you will forget how much you liked the antlers you have today."

"Balamoose's antlers grow so big that they are not called antlers. They are called panache. That is the word people use when they want to say with great style and daring. They say you have panache. You will have a great panache."

Standor said: "My friend, part of growing up is learning that sometimes you have to give up something to get another thing you want. It will be a good thing for you to give up your panache. In return you will be free. You will be able to do many nice things that you cannot do now. That will be better than spinning around a stem. That will be good."

That convinced the balamoose. He agreed. "Yes, I think you are right. I am ready to remove the suspenders. They are all twisted, will you help me?"

The suspenders were twisted everywhere. They were twisted around the stem many more times than many. One part was also hung up on a branch. The braces were everywhere. It looked like it was going to be very hard to free the balamoose.

It would have been easier if the children had cut the stem of the lolly of the volly. They would not do that. It was such a pretty and sweet-smelling flower. Its stem was what gave it life. It would be wrong to kill the lolly of the volley to free the balamoose.

It was not the flower's fault if the balamoose had hung its suspenders on its petals. The lolly of the volly had had as much trouble as the balamoose. The children decided to be very careful not to hurt the lolly of the volly as they worked to free the balamoose.

The horse of two feathers and the zoom-by helped. Standor and the children worked very hard and long. Finally, their work was done. Steerwarp, awooswish and wrapoonk, the suspenders swimpked free

The balamoose was free.

Plunk, stampkt and splunk, the antlers fell of.

It is a good thing the horse of two feathers did not have long toes. If he had, the antlers would have smashed at least two and a half of his toes.

Everybody looked on the ground at the fallen panache. The balamoose was right. It looked great. The panache actually looked like a balamoose without the balamoose's body under it.

The balamoose was sad to see them alone on the ground. His head felt naked. That made him sad.

Coral was the first to look up at the balamoose. She said: "Look! Look! Mr. Balamoose look where the antlers were. Are these two little horns on you head?"

"My!" Yelled the balamoose. He was terrified. "I have become a devil! Oh - What troubles!"

"No." Said Standor who was calm. "Look carefully. I think Coral was right. These are the beginning of a new panache. You will soon have a new set of antlers."

No one had ever seen a balamoose skip and hop with as much joy before. No one had seen a balamoose grin so happily before.

He was free and new antlers were growing.

"Ooo thank you. Ooo thank you. Ooo, Ooo thank you." He yelled as he skipped away in the florest. It was the first time in a very long time that the balamoose was free to go far from the lolly of the volly. "I am so happy!"

The children were very happy that the balamoose was happy. He was now free to act like a balamoose and look like one too. The balamoose was a double winner. The balamoose was being a balamoose. That is what a balamoose should be.

"I am so proud of you." Said Standor. "Again, you have done another very good thing. You have helped us solve a great problem. I am also happy that you did that without hurting the lolly of the volly."

"So am I." Said the lolly of the volly. She was happy to be rid of the balamoose hanging from her petals.

The children were happy to have helped. They felt as happy as people feel happy when they are with happy people.

On the Way

The horse of two feathers and the zoom-by had helped the children free the balamoose. They too were very happy. The feathers of the horse's head wiggled with joy. The zoom-by was so happy he was giggling. He was giggling so hard that with each giggle his stripes wiggled and changed place.

At the end the zoom-by's stripes were all mixed up. They looked like Z's. It was right that the stripes of a zoom-by would look like Z's. That made him very proud and happy.

The children and their animal friends were so happy that they felt like having a picnic party.

They started to lay a blanket in the shade of a pretty orange 'glad I am a yola'.

The zoom-by was about to invite all the ants he knew - and he knew many of them. He knew the Antarctic, the antifreeze, the antenna and the 'anter at your own risks'. Ants like to go to picnics. He also knew the antisocial, but he is the only ant that does not like picnics.

From far away an impatience shouted: "What are you doing? There is no time to lose. Get going."

That reminded Standor who, being as wise as only Standor was wise, reminded the children that they wanted to see Rainbow Falls that day. He wanted to celebrate as much as the children. But he knew that seeing Rainbow Falls could be as good as any fifteen of the best parties or four of the best picnics.

The children agreed with Standor. The zoom-by was a little disappointed that he could not invite all his ant friends to a picnic. He really wanted to show them his new Z stripes. Everyone knows that zoom-bys like to show off.

It was all right to want to show off his new Zs. It was like showing off new clothes. Everybody likes doing that. For the zoom-by, it was the very first time he had new clothes. That made the occasion very special.

Everyone agreed that once they got to Rainbow Falls the zoom-by could show his new Zs to anyone who would be there. That made the zoom-by happy.

This time the children rode the zoom-by and Standor got on the horse of two feathers. They held on very tight. They knew that the ride was going to be a very fast one. It was a fast ride. They traveled faster than fast. They rode almost as fast as two times faster than fast. They even passed a "gazool" and a "gazam" who were already running as fast as they could. They also passed a "sidewalk runner" being chased by a "cayoot" in a kayak. They also passed a "turrettle" and a "smail". But that did not count. The turrettle and the smail were going the other way.

They went directly to the Rainbow Falls. They stopped only once. That was to say hello to their friends, Balboa and Cadwallader, the nicey tertiums.

Both of them were very happy and excited to see the children again. They would have danced had their roots not been so deep into the ground.

They said they had written 63 poems for their mother since they had last seen the children. They were very proud of their poems. They wanted to recite all of them to the children. But Standor explained that the children were in a hurry and could not stop very long.

The impatience gasped: "We don't have time to lose. Get going."

Coral and Emorix said they could listen to only one - the best one - then they would have to go.

Balboa suggested they recite the poem they called "Its nicey to be a nicey" that she had written. Cadwallader wanted to recite the one he had made up. It was called "Its not nasty not to be a nasty".

The nicey tertiums talked about it for a little while, each wanted to recite his own poem. Finally, they agreed that they would recite a new one that they would call "Its nicey not to be nasty".

Its nicey not to be a nasty
Its not nasty to be a nicey
Hip Hip Hooray
Hip Hip Hooray

We are not nasties
Because we are nicies
We are nice nicies
because we are not nasty nasties

Hip Hip Hooray
Hip Hip Hooray
The other day we were nasties
but today we are nicies

Hip Hip Hooray
Hip Hip Hooray
Hip Hip Hooray

Hip Hip Hooray.

No one said that it was a silly poem. They had all been thought to be polite by their mother.

Everybody, even the horse of two feathers who had been their prisoner thanked the Nicey Tertiums for their poem. Maybe they thanked them because the poem was finished.

They all said: "Goodbye."

The nicey tertiums said: "Tata tooraloo, we will see you."

The impatience said: "let's get going."

The children, Standor, the horse of two feathers and the zoom-by left for the Rainbow Falls. They did not just go to the Rainbow Falls; they zoomed with both feathers flying. Coral said: "Stop! Look up there!"

They stopped. The children had never seen anything like this.

The Entrance to Rainbow Falls

I can tell you that they were not at Rainbow Falls yet. However, just over the giant white chrisentemmaximum, the children could see a rainbow going up towards the sky. Then, they could see another rainbow following the first one. Then there was another rainbow. In the few minutes that they stood still, the children saw seven different rainbows shooting through the top of the flowers, towards different directions in the sky. They were like rockets. Better still, it was like fireworks!

Standor explained that Rainbow Falls is the beginning of the rainbow. This is where rainbows are born. There are many rainbows in the whole world. Sometimes there is a rainbow at your home and another one in China. There might even be a rainbow in the middle of the sea. Even Santa Claus likes to enjoy rainbows in the North Pole.

There may even be rainbows at the South Pole. I am nor sure of that. I have not heard of anyone who has ever seen a rainbow at the South Pole. That may be because no one lives there.

Standor explained that the children were seeing the birth of the rainbows. "We call it the 'Rainbownaissance'." He spoke.

The children and the zoom-by, who had never been at Rainbow Falls before, were standing in the middle of the path with their mouth wide open. They were not advancing. They would have stood there and watched the rainbow show for a very long time. But the horse of two feathers had already been at Rainbow Falls. He spoke. He told them that they should go forward quickly. There were many more fantastropic things to see. "Let's go! Let's go! Let's go quickly!" He said. An impatience agreed.

The horse was so excited - he started trembling. He looked like a bowl of Jell-O in an earthquake. The children and Standor became worried. There was so much shaking. Maybe the horse of two feathers would stop sticking together. But he did stick together. That proved how solid horses of two feathers are built. No doubt about that now! "Let's go! Let's go! Let's go quickly!" He said again.

Standor agreed. He said that no matter how much the Rainbow shoot was spectapeculiar, the best had yet to come. Once at Rainbow Falls, it would be even better than that.

Everybody started moving forward. They were not running. They were walking on the tip of their toes as if they were afraid to disturb nature. It is easy to imagine a horse of two feathers walking on the tip of his toes. With his fancy blue and green feathers, he already almost looked like a ballet dancer. It is harder to imagine a zoom-by zooming slowly on the tip of his toes.

Zoom-bys don't have toes.

Emorix was the first to turn the corner. "Halt! Who goes there?" Said a gentle baby voice.

Emorix looked all around him. Coral looked all around Emorix. They looked at each other. They saw each other – besides that they saw nothing.

"Halt! Who goes there?"

They looked at the horse of two feathers. He was giggling. They looked at Standor. His eyes were smiling. He nodded his head and pointed his eyes to the ground around the children

The entrance to Rainbow Falls is guarded.
Will the children be able to enter?

No wonder they had not seen anything. They had not looked that carefully on the ground.

"Halt! Who goes there?" The voice came from a little baby. It was actually smaller than a little baby. It was a very little baby. As little as a baby could be. The very little baby was behind a teeny-weeny gate and ahead of two rows of what looked like little baby bunnies. The children were not sure. They had learned that you never can be sure about what goes on in the Florest of Ronkledongding.

"Halt! Who goes there?"

I am Coral and this is my brother Emorix. We are with our friends, Standor, the horse of two feathers and the zoom-by. I believe you already know Standor and the horse of two feathers. They have been here before. We have never been here before, nor has the zoom-by.

"What is the password?"

Emorix said: "I don't know the password"

"Ah! That is the password. You can enter." The baby opened the gate.

Coral and Emorix stepped forward.

"Halt! Not so fast!" Emorix can go forward, he knew the password. You, Coral, you did not say the password. You cannot enter.

"Ask me." Said Coral.

"What is the password?"

Coral had a big problem. If she said: "I don't know the password." She would lie. She knew the password. She knew it was "I don't know the password."

She knew it was bad to lie. She did not want to lie. But she had to say: "I don't know the password." To be allowed to enter. What a problem! What was she going to do? Lie and enter or not lie and stay outside the gate. She thought a lot about it. What was she to do?

Standor watched carefully. Was Coral about to tell a lie?

Coral remembered the ant sniffer. She smiled. She knew what to do. She would be precise. She said: "The password is: 'I don't know the password'". She had said it and she had not lied. Standor was impressed. He smiled.

The baby opened the gate for Coral.

Standor and the zoom-by each had to give the password before they were allowed to pass the gate.

Although he knew that the password was "I don't know the password." The baby would not let the horse of two feathers enter.

"You are an impostor!" she said.

"No! I am not an impostor. I am a horse of two feathers. Look on top of my head."

The children had said that the horse of two feathers had been there before. The baby thought it was a lie. She did not recognize him. The horse of two feathers had to explain that when he came to Rainbow Falls, he had been a horse of one feather who could not stick together. It is only after drinking the water at Rainbow Falls that he had become a horse of two feathers. Of course, he had left through the departure gate. The baby, who was always at the entrance gate, did not see him leave. The baby understood. She let the horse of two feathers enter.

Coral asked the baby who she was. What she was doing.

I am Sabine. "I am the SUCORAFEG. That means Supreme Commander of the Rainbow Falls Entrance Guard. This is my guard. Together we make sure that only good people who know the password enter Rainbow Falls." She said as she pointed at the bunnies.

Emorix said. "These are cute bunnies."

"They are not cute bunnies. They are "bumpies". They have been trained. They can guard anything. Specially, they can guard the entrance gate to the Rainbow Falls."

Emorix had trouble seeing how a baby and some baby bumpies could guard anything. He asked. "How do you do that?"

Sabine replied is a very low voice. "It is a secret. It is very hush-hush. We only speak about it in a hush-hush voice. Sometimes our voice would be even lower than that, but babies cannot speak in deep low voices. Sometimes we put our head under the blankets to speak about it. Sometimes we speak in code. The code is called baby talk. We do not want anyone to know our secret plan. We only tell it to those who ask. I am glad you asked."

Sabine looked around her to see if anyone else was listening. There was an ant that could be listening. She asked Standor to please put the ant in his pants so the ant could not hear. Standor, who is always nice, smiled and said: "Yes, with pleasure." He was used to it. This happened every time he came to the entrance at Rainbow Falls. Standor once had thousands of ants in his pants. At first, he found that they tickled a lot. Later, he had a special pocket made to hold them. That stopped the tickling. Now he had solved the problem. Instead of having thousand of ants in his pants, Standor had thousands of pants. He put one ant in each pair. It was easier. However, when he had ants in his pants, Standor had to be careful to stay away from the ant snifter - very far away.

Now that she was certain that the ant could not hear, Sabine explained that guarding the entrance gate was an important job. No one wanted litterbugs, bandits and other baddies to come to Rainbow Falls. What if they stopped the making of the rainbows?

There were many tricks to defend the falls.

The first trick was to place a pot of gold at the end of the rainbow. Bandits would go there. They like to steal gold. They would not come to Rainbow Falls. It is at the beginning of the Rainbow.

The second trick was very sneaky. Many rainbows were sent to other pretty waterfalls outside the Florest of Ronkledongding. When people first saw them, they called the waterfalls 'Rainbow Falls'. There are so many waterfalls called Rainbow Falls that bad bandits would have great trouble finding the very right one. The Rainbow Falls where the children had arrived was the only one that was very right.

The third trick was the password trick. No one told the password to the litterbugs and to the bandits. Also, bandits rarely tell the truth. If a bandit came to the gate and was asked the password, he would never say: "I don't know the password." That would be telling the truth. That is why bandits don't know the password and cannot guess it.

The fourth trick was the gate. Sabine admitted that the gate was very small. Babies and bumpies are not big enough to build big gates. If they could, they would not be big enough to open and close the big gate. But the gate was still a good trick. It was so small that the baddies would probably not see it. They would trip on it.

When a baddy tripped on the gate, the bumpies would jump and hop on top of him. They were trained to do that. The jumping was the fifth trick.

The sixth trick was the best of all. If a bandit came and tried to enter, Sabine would cry. No one, not even bandits like to hear teeny, little babies cry. That would stop them. If they did not stop at first, Sabine would continue to cry. She would even cry louder. Babies can cry for seven hours without hurting their lungs. No one can stand hearing a baby cry for seven hours without hurting his or her ears. Less than one hour would break the heart of most people.

Sabine told them that those were all the secret tricks. The children could see that the tricks would probably work.

Even if they did not work, it was not too bad. No one is capable of seeing Rainbow Falls and remain bad. Rainbow Falls can make the baddest, meanest, most grunchypiest bandit become good.

Coral thanked Sabine. Emorix thanked her as well.

A nearby impatience said: "We have wasted enough time. Let's get going."

Rainbow Falls

There is no doubt that the children could not have been able to take their eyes away from the splendor of the falls if it had not been for the beauty of the Rainbow Princess.

"My friends, I would like you to meet my sister, Patricia, the Rainbow Princess. Patricia, this is Coral, Emorix and the zoomby. You already know Standor and the horse of two feathers."

"I am pleased to meet you. My brother and I have been following your adventure since you arrived. You have made many friends. You have done much good. You can be proud of yourselves. I am proud of you."

Her voice sounded like a smile.

Emorix thought that she was so marvelous. He liked her just as much as he liked William. This is as much as everything else plus 50 times "too many". Everybody loved the Princess Patricia. She gave a big hug to Standor and complimented the horse of two feathers about his new feathers. She said they complemented his mane very well."

The horse explained that although they were blue and green this was okay. Blue and green can be together outside the washing machine. Bluelets are blue and green. They are outside the washing machine. He blushed and said that in principle, the feathers were now his principal features.

Standor was pleased that the princess and the horse of two feathers each knew when to use "complement" and "compliment" and when to use "principal" and "principle". He thought it was a good sign.

Princess Patricia looked radiant. Her eyes had a smile as pretty as the smile on her face. She wore a long white dress. She had a pretty crown made of petals and pearls from the river on her head. In her left hand she had a magic wand carved from the thorns of a potrose. Her shoes were made from dewdrops collected from the petal of a lolly of the volley early in the morning when they glisten in the sun. The light from the smile in her eyes sparkled against the dew of her shoes.

The Rainbow Princess sat on a throne made by combining three moonbeams, the twinkles of seventeen stars and the softness of six snowflakes. She sat on a cushion of sunlight. There were eight beautiful peacock-a-doodle-do's around her on the ground. They lay down quietly as if sitting in their nest. Their feathers were spread out like a fan. They faced the throne and the Rainbow Princess. Six of the peacock-a-doodle-do's had a pretty triangular hat on their heads. Two did not. The hats were made of mirrors.

The throne was immediately beside the pond. Resting at the edge of the pond was a very beautiful and smart looking fish. "Is this your fish? It looks very friendly." Said Coral. Patricia replied: "It is not a fish. It is a mammal just like you and me. It is a dollfine. I like her very much. After my brother, she is my best friend. She helps me make rainbows. When we are not busy, we play domino. Sometimes, I win. Sometimes, she wins. Every time, we have fun." Coral nodded. She understood. She even understood that you could still have fun even when you do not win. That is a hard thing to understand.

The area around Princess Patricia's throne was a "Gee golly - great galoshes! I have not ever seen anything as splendid as this" sight.

The prettiest things were Patricia's intentions. They were clear. They lay open on the table in front of her. They were all good and sincere. It was clear that the Princess wanted to do well. She wanted to make everyone happy.

No one has ever seen something so pretty. The children and their friends were very happy to meet the Rainbow Princess.

Emorix was very taken. He could hardly speak.

The zoom-by said: "Wha wha wha zoom! Wow! I have never seen… Wow wow wow! Why do they call you the Rainbow Princess?" I think he was excited.

Patricia explained that she had two jobs. Every morning she made her bed. The rest of the time her job was to make rainbows.

She and Prince William discussed whether a place needed a rainbow to cheer the children who lived there. If they thought it was a good idea, Princess Patricia would make the rainbow while William made the preparations to send the rainbows to where they were needed.

"You can make rainbows? Real rainbows - Can we see you make one?" Asked Coral. She likes to be shown.

Again, Patricia explained that Rainbow Falls was where all rainbows in the whole world are born. Rainbow Falls is always the beginning of the rainbow. That never changes. What changes is the end of the rainbow – the place where the pot of gold is. She also explained that rainbow making was a serious matter. Rainbows were made only when they were needed to cheer someone. She could not make a rainbow just to show Coral how rainbows were made. Coral and her friends would have to wait.

Coral understood and asked as politely as she could whether she could watch Princess Patricia make the next rainbow.

Patricia smiled making many sparkles reflect on her shoes. She said she would be happy if Coral and Emorix and their friends watched her when she made the next rainbow. The wait would not be long. Sometimes they make hundreds of rainbows in the same day.

Coral smiled and said thank you.

The zoom-by was so excited that he could hardly zoom still.

The magic at Rainbow Falls.

The Rainbow Princess and her brother make rainbows.

Don't you wish they were sending one to you now?

Making Rainbows

The children sat on a bench made of the roots of a truelip and waited. They waited for quite a while. They were not bored. There were so many pretty things to see. So many new sounds to listen to. They were not hungry. William had given each of them a drink of choconut milk. They were not tired. The adventure was too exiting to be tired. From their bench they could see the whole area around Rainbow Falls.

They could see the guards. They could see the grand-dogs and Poke sniffing. They could see all the pretty flowers and hear the pretty birds. They could hear the peep and whistle of the choirs. Still, the children were in a hurry to see the birth of a rainbow.

They were looking at the monkbees swinging from flower to flower when they saw a white dove come down and land beside the pond. The dove cooed and three birds that looked like penguins came out of an igloo beside the frozen part of the pond. The birds were penguists. They started skating on the ice.

"Ah! It is time to go." Said William. "Someone needs a rainbow." He hurried down the stairs to the place where the penguists were skating.

"What is happening?" Asked Emorix.

Patricia explained that the beautiful white bird that had flown to the side of the river was not a dove as the children had taught. It was a love. Love's language sometimes is very hard to understand. It is often misunderstood. When it is misunderstood, it causes much trouble. They were lucky that the penguists understood the language of love perfectly well. They could hear it with their ears. They could read it with their eyes. They could feel it with their hearts. There was one problem. As you know, penguists cannot speak.

As often happens in life and always happens in the Florest of Ronkledongding, there was a problem but there was also a solution. In the case of the penguists they could write. Looking at a penguists you cannot tell that they can write. They have stubby wings instead of hands. It is hard to hold a pen with stubby wings. Penguists do not write with a pen. They write with their feet. Actually, they write with the ice skates on their feet. Their feet are webbed. So are the skates. They are the only animals that can write with web skates.

Patricia explained that this was why a part of the pond was kept frozen. The penguists needed a writing tablet. The children nodded that they understood. The zoom-by tried to imagine how much fun it would be to zoom on the ice. He smiled at the idea until he remembered that he did not know how to skate. He would zoom fall on the ice, zoom fall on his behind and perhaps zoom fall on his beside.

The children watched carefully as the love whispered to the penguists. After a while the penguists smiled a big beeky-toothy penguist grin and nodded. They put on their scarf and their mittens and began skating.

They skated an "A", then there was an "R", then another "A", then an "I", then a "B" then an "O" then a "W". It took two penguists to trace the "w" on the ice. The children read aloud as each new word appeared on the ice.

A....RAINBOW....IS....NEEDED....OVER....SIMON"S HOUSE....It....IS....RAINING....HE....CANNOT....GO....... OUT....AND....RIDE....HIS....BICYCLE....THAT....MAKES ....HIM....SAD.

The children wondered if Simon was their cousins. The one who lives far away.

William was very good at reading and writing. He took a writing pad and a pen from his bag. He wrote the message down. He checked his new watch and wrote the time on the paper.

Next, William went to the top of the hill on Point William. That was the name of the point where he worked. He started a blue computer on the table beside his chair. He read on the screen. He found out where Simon lived. He also checked whether he had been good, had done all his homework, went to bed without complaining and kept his room tidy. He had. He printed that.

William went up the path and talked to Princess Patricia. They decided that Simon would get a rainbow to make him happy. He loves going to the park on their bicycles.

Patricia got from her throne and went to a treasure chest. William warned the children not to get too close to the treasure chest. Four tall and very beautiful flowers planted around the chest guarded it. These flowers were "Meanest Why Traps". They were the last level of security. If anyone except William, Patricia, Sabine or the grand-dogs and Poke got close to the chest, the Meanest Why Traps would ask "Why?" If the answer was not right – and it never was - they would ask "why?" again. They would continue to ask "why" until the intruder would apologize and leave. There are very few things worse than being asked "Why?" when you don't know "Why". One of them is to be asked "Why" again when you still don't know "Why". It is enough to make your nose drip, your ears twitch, and your toes curl.

William took one of the keys from his tool belt and opened the treasure chest. Patricia took a beautiful crystal bowl from the chest. She returned to her throne and William returned to Point William.

Princess Patricia placed the Bowl on a clear glass table in front of her throne. She poured some water from Rainbow Falls into the bowl. She stood up. She dipped her magic wan into the water. She pointed her wand towards a beautiful Flower. It was a "pit-a-tuna". The sun reflected on the crystal of her wand and changed the color of the water in the bowl. It turned in a pure violet color.

The zoom-by looked and said: "Ho my!"

Patricia went back to the chest and took a second crystal bowl. Again, she placed it on the table in front of her throne. Again, she filled the bowl with water from Rainbow Falls. Standing up, she dipped her wand into the water. She pointed her wand towards a "blue belle". The sun reflecting on the crystal of her wand took the color from the blue belle and poured it into the water. The water became a deep blue. It glistened as a baby's blue eyes. The blue was deep but as soft as powder.

The zoom-by looked again and said: "Ho my!"

Patricia went back to the chest and took another crystal bowl. She placed it on the table in front of her throne. Again, she filled the bowl with water from Rainbow Falls. She stood up. She dipped her wand into the water. She pointed her wand towards a beautiful Flower. It was a huge "road-a-tantrum". The sun reflected on the crystal of her wand and changed the color of the water in the bowl. The water became green. It turned into a green as clear as the green of the road-a-tantrum.

The zoom-by looked again and said: "Ho my my!"

Patricia went back to the chest for the fourth time. She took another crystal bowl. She did as she did before. This time she pointed her wand towards a fun flower. The sun reflected on the crystal of her wand and changed the color of the water in the bowl. This time the water became a bright yellow, as bright as the sun, as soft as butter.

The zoom-by looked again and said: "Ho my! Ho my!"

Patricia took a fifth crystal bowl from the chest. She placed it on the table in front of her throne. She dipped her wand into the water from Rainbow Falls that she had poured into the bowl. She pointed her wand towards a nicey tertium. The water became a vivid orange, as cool as an orange Popsicle. It made Emorix think of Halloween.

The zoom-by looked again and said: "Ho ho my my!"

Princess Patricia went back to the chest and took another crystal bowl. This time her wand borrowed the color from a potrose. It turned the water deep red, red like a heart on Saint Valentine Day or red like Santa Claus' suit. It was as red as a holiday!

The zoom-by looked again and said: "Ho my! Ho my my!"

Patricia went back to the chest and took another crystal bowl. This one was different. It was clear but made of a very dark blue glass. She placed the bowl it on the table in front of her throne. Again, she filled the bowl with water from Rainbow Falls. She stood up. She dipped her wand into the water. She pointed her wand towards a beautiful Flower. It was a maganifficient "in-I-go" plant. The sun reflected on the crystal of her wand and changed the color of the water in the bowl. The water became very dark blue just like the glass in the bowl. It was a very different blue than the water in the second bowl. This was a much richer blue. It was a dark blue like the taste of a chocolate and grape sandwich.

The zoom-by looked again and said: "Ho my! Ho my! Ho ho!"

Patricia took a last bowl from the chest. This time she pointed at a lolly of the volley. She turned the Rainbow Falls water into a pure white liquid. It looked as refreshing as cold milk.

The zoom-by looked again and said: "Ho my! My my my my my ho ho!"

Princess Patricia had eight beautiful crystal bowls in front of her. Each bowl was filled with a liquid of a different color.

The zoom-by looked again and said nothing. He was speechless.

While the princess was changing the color of the Rainbow Falls water, William who is very good at mathematics was busy at his computer doing complex calculations. He looked at a map and calculated the distance between Rainbow Falls and Sabrina's and Simon's home. It was over 4000 camel-otters. He calculated how fast the rainbow would have to travel to reach their home in time for them to ride their bicycles. He found out he would have to send it at 3 times normal rainbow speed of thirty-seven otter-camels per grin time. A grin time is the time it takes a child to grin when he sees his mother or a yummy desert, a funny thing or a birthday present. It is not a very long time.

The hardest calculation was the height of the rainbow. Rainbowologists know that the colors of the rainbow are seen when there is an angle of 40 to 42 degrees between the sun, the drop of water and the person who looks at the rainbow. They think it is the light of the sun that goes through the droplets of water that make the colors. We know that the colors come from the flowers of the Florest of Ronkledongding.

William was a champion rainbowologist. He knew that the rainbow had to be at the right height if Simon and Sabrina were to see it. That was a lot of very complicated calculations. He wrote all the results on his computer. It is a good thing that he paid attention in school. It is a good thing that he did all his homework carefully. It is a good thing that he studied his tables very hard. It is a good thing that he knew how to count without using his fingers and his toes. The numbers were so big that even if he were to invite all his uncles and all his aunts and all his friends and all their uncles and all their aunts, there would still not be enough toes and fingers to count all the numbers.

To get the proper angle, William had two choices. He could wait until Sabrina and Simon grew taller or he could lower the height of the rainbow. He decided not to wait. Now it was time to make the rainbow. Sabrina and Simon were waiting.

William told the grand-dogs and Poke to look up. He explained that one day someone said that rainbows exist only if someone sees them. The friends at Rainbow Falls did not think this was the case. However, they were not about to take any chances. One of the jobs of the grand-dogs and Poke was to be the witnesses. They looked at every rainbow born at Rainbow Falls. That way, all rainbows were seen as they left. Making sure that a rainbow would be seen was not a waste of time. They are so pretty. They should always be seen. The grand-dogs and Poke made certain that there would be no chance that a rainbow would be wasted. Even the mother of the grand dogs and the mother of Poke agreed that this was a very important job.

The grand-dogs and Poke were ready. They were sitting facing the falls. Princess Patricia stood up. She put on a beautiful robe of purple "pita-unia" petals sprinkled with the gold stars that shine on black truelips at dawn when the sun sparkles on them. It was tied around her neck with the black diamond seed of a nicey tertium and a chain made from a "merry gold". She looked absolutely splendifremendous. Of course, Emorix already knew she would.

The rainbow Princess placed each bowl on a plate of dizzies held in the air by three giant "chummingbirds" hovering as if they were multi-colored helicopters.

William checked the calculations he had written on his computer. He told the Princess where to place the bowl filled with violet water. The he told her where to place the bowl filled with blue water. He did the same for each of the other bowls, the green bowl, the yellow bowl, the orange bowl, the red bowl, the dark blue bowl and the white bowl.

Once each bowl was in its proper place, the Rainbow Princess guided each of the eight peacock-a-doodle-do's so they would each be under one of the bowls. The peacock-a-doodle-do's looked carefully at the ground. Maybe they were looking for something to eat.

Patricia whispered to her dollfine. The dollfine raced around the pound. She jumped in front of the Princess. She made a very big splash at the bottom of the Rainbow Fall. There were many "slapmon" fish asleep in the pond. The splash scared the slapmon fish. In panic, they raced towards the fall. They jumped very high. They tried to climb up the Rainbow Falls. That made many more splashes. There were drops of water all over. The sound of the splashes made the peacock-a-doodle-do's look up.

Then it happened.

The Rainbow Princess took a ray of sunlight with her wand. She made that ray bounce on the water curtain falling from rainbow Falls. The light reflected against the droplets. It bounced down towards the bowls. The light stabbed through the colored water in the bowl. Each ray took the color of the water. Then each ray reflected on the mirrors on the head of the peacock-a-doodle-do under each bowl.

First there was a violet arch raising into the sky. Then there was a blue one right beside it. Then there was a green arch reflecting from the mirror high into the sky. A bright yellow band shot in the air. Then there was an orange arch followed by a beautiful red band.

There were two other rays. The dark blue one and a creamy white ray. They did not bounce up and form an arch. When they penetrated through the bowl, the last two rays bounced on the head of each peacock-a-doodle-do's that did not have mirrors. These beautiful light rays were lost on the ground. The colored water stayed in the bowls.

Coral and Emorix had just seen the birth of a rainbow.

The children were amazed. Making rainbows was a very complicated thing to do. They were happy they had seen that. They had seen a miracle.

The zoom-by was still speechless.

Patricia explained that the dark blue crystal bowl was "indigo", Long ago "Indigo" was recognized as a separate color in the rainbow spectrum. There was indigo in rainbows.

Today there is a problem. Because the peacock-a-doodle-do under the indigo bowl has lost the mirror on his hat, there is no reflection. No reflection from the hat means that not any indigo shoots in the sky. It means no indigo in rainbows. Patricia said: "It is most unfortunate he did not take care of his mirror. One should always take care not to lose things. Indigo was the strongest color in the rainbow. It was a solid color."

The Rainbow Princess also explained that the peacock-a-doodle-do under the white bowl never had a mirror on top of his hat. That is probably why there has never been a rainbow with white polka dots.

Coral and Emorix congratulated the Rainbow Princess and her brother. They thanked them very much.

Standor was pleased that the children had seen the birth of a Rainbow.

The horse of two feathers and the zoom-by were also very happy.

The zoom by told everybody he was speechless. He and the horse of two feathers had never seen something so beautiful. They asked William whether they could stay and help making rainbows. William said that yes, they could.

The Way Home

Emorix was about to ask whether they could stay as well when Coral reminded him that they had to get home. Their parents and Mokka were worried. They would be waiting.

Coral had an idea. She had a very good idea.

She asked William whether the rainbow had gone to Sabrina's and Simon's home. William explained that the rainbow had arched right over their home. He had made the right calculations.

Coral asked whether it was possible to send a rainbow over anyone's home – even to her own home. William told her that he could calculate the direction and height of a rainbow to go anywhere in the world – even to her home.

Coral explained her thinking.

Emorix and Coral remembered they had come down the blue arch of a rainbow to land in the Florest of Ronkledongding. Perhaps it would be possible to go back home using a rainbow. They could hold on very hard until they came above their house. William could aim the rainbow so it would be very low and directly above the trampoline above their home. Then they could let go and bounce their way back home.

Patricia was sad that the children wanted to leave. She wanted to invite them to play a game with the dollfine. William was also sad. He wanted to show them all his tools. He wanted Emorix to help him fix a broken caramel that was missing a bite and mend a rock that had no teeth.

Patricia admitted that it was a good plan. There was a problem with it. She reminded the children that the blue band of the rainbow was very slippery. The children would not be able to hang on to it.

Emorix suggested that they could hold on to another arch. Perhaps they could hang onto the red or the orange band. William was the one who told the children that the other bands of the rainbow were not very strong. None of them were strong enough to hold the children. The plan would not work.

"Wait a minute, I have another idea." Said Coral. "Did you not say that the indigo band was made of a solid blue? Is it not strong enough?"

It is true; indigo is a very strong blue. It could hold the children. The Rainbow Princess reminded the children that rainbows did not have indigo bands. The peacock-a-doodle-do under the indigo bowl had lost its mirror. That plan would not work.

"Ah, but it could." Said Emorix. "What we have to do is place one of the other peacock-a-doodle-do, one with a mirror under the indigo bowl. Perhaps the one that is normally under the blue bowl. That could work."

Standor smiled. The children had discovered the secret of going home. They knew "The Way Out". He was very proud of them.

Everybody got very busy.

William made his calculations. He asked the children to tell him where the trampoline was. To be sure, William made his calculations twice.

The grand-dogs and Poke took their position to witness the rainbow.

The Rainbow Princess filled all the bowls with colored Rainbow Falls water. She placed the eight peacock-a-doodle-do's under the bowls. This time she placed the blue peacock-a-doodle-do – the one with a mirror, under the indigo bowl. She placed the indigo peacock-a-doodle-do, the one without a mirror, under the blue bowl.

Standor suggested that the children make gloves from the leaves of a little "clinging vine". The leaves can climb over anything. They are sticky. They would help the children to hang on very tight to the indigo band.

When everything was ready the children said goodbye to all their friends. Everybody was sad that the children were leaving. Everybody was happy that the children were going to see their parents.

Standor reminded the children that they had flipped from head to toe when they came. They had tripped on the rainbow. They were now still upside down. Everything in the Florest of Ronkledongding was upside down. If they left the way, they are they would arrive home headfirst. They should leave standing on their head. That way they would land on their feet.

It is a good thing that the children knew how to do somersaults. They could almost stand on their head. The horse of two feathers and William helped by holding their feet.

The children placed themselves upside down just above the peacock-a-doodle-do that was under the indigo bowl. They held each other very tight.

Princess Patricia whispered to the dollfine. She began making the special rainbow.

She made the violet arch.

She made the indigo band. The children grabbed it, with their feet and with their hands. They rose into the air. The children were on their way home.

The Rainbow Princess made the green, the yellow, the orange and the red band.

There was no arch when she reflected the sun in the blue band. That peacock-a-doodle-do did not have a mirror.

Of course, there were no white polka dots either.

There was the most beautiful rainbow anyone had ever seen. That is all. It was a rare rainbow that had an indigo band. A very special rainbow.

It was a rainbow with two wonderful children riding on the indigo band, flying home.

Standor yelled: "Be careful!" William waved. Patricia blew them sweet kisses.

The children waved and blew kisses back.

Rainbows fly very fast. They fly just as fast as Santa Claus. It was not very long before the children recognized their town. The first thing the saw was the fair. Then they saw their home. William had calculated right. They were very low and just above the trampoline.

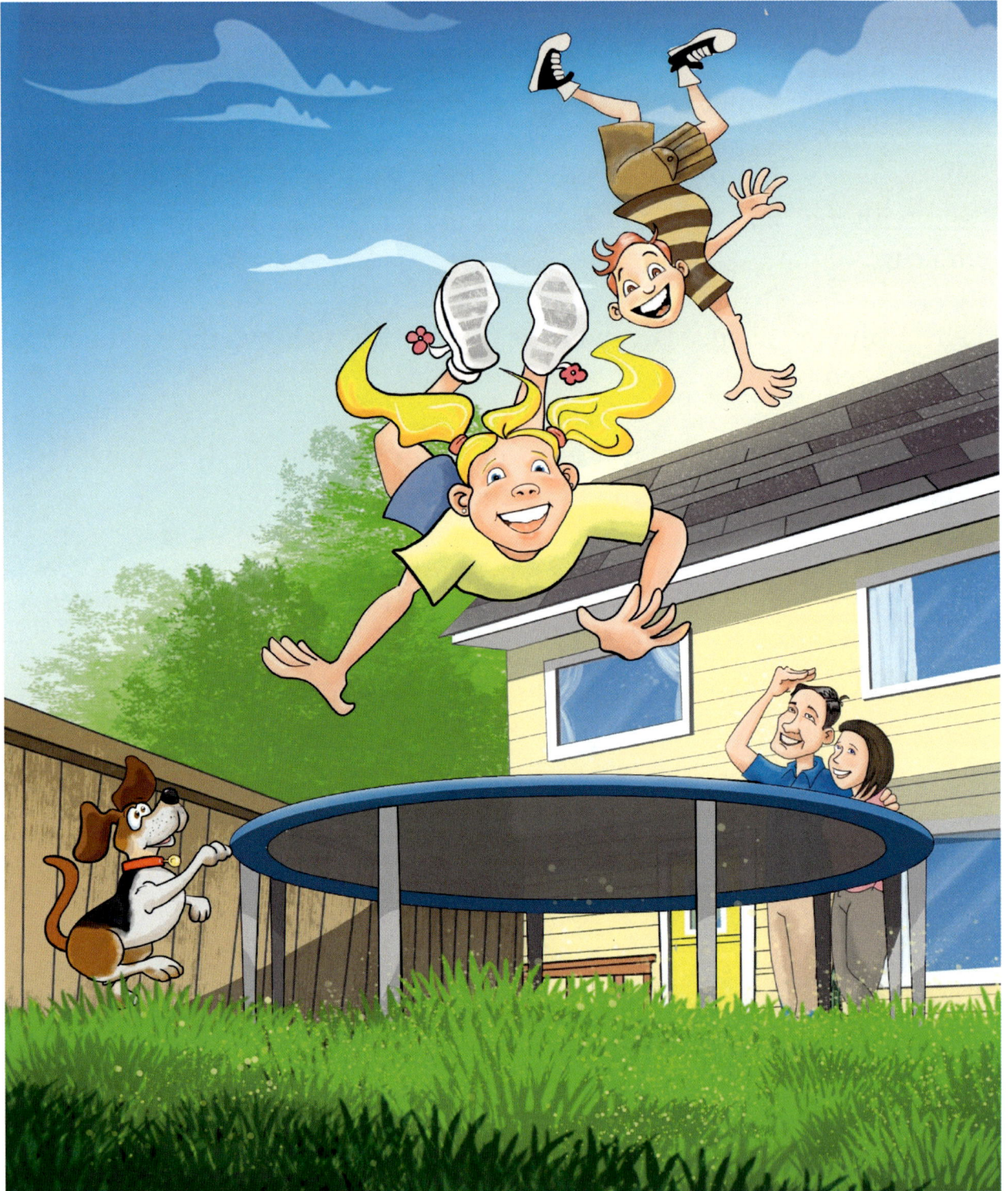

Home Sweet Home

They opened their hand and let go. They bounced forty-seven and three and one half times on the trampoline. Then they bounced once more, just for fun, before they could stop.

Mokka was the first to notice them. She barked and wagged her tail. She was happy.

The parents came out to see why Mokka was barking. They saw their children. They were very, very, very happy.

Emorix and Coral were back home. They had a wonderful story to tell. They were happy.

Whenever you see a rainbow, look carefully. Look where the blue band is supposed to be. If instead of a blue band you see an indigo arch it could be that someone is coming back from a wonderful adventure in the Florest of Ronkledongding. It could be because that is the way out.

Manufactured by Amazon.ca
Bolton, ON